WOOD SONG

A WYNN VALE TALE

MARY LAY

CONTENTS

1904

HE COULD HEAR HER singing. It was enough to drive a man to drink, that sweet voice with its dusky deepness. Edmund had every right to be there. One day he would take over as Bailiff, Brickham Roach would surely not last too many more winters in the Vale, but as the Bailiff's Man, Edmund could go anywhere he chose on the Marchett Estate whether he had papers to serve or not.

Still, she sang. Did she know he was watching her? How could she, he was a good one hundred feet away and crouched low in the dip of a beech tree's roots. His knees were damp. He should stand. Should move on and away. He could not.

Betony Trow knew he was there all right. It was all she could do to keep the mirth from infecting the tune she sang. It was as well that Edmund Prentice was a Bailiff's Man as he would never have succeeded as a poacher. He was up-wind of her, and his scent of leather and tar had announced his presence some minutes earlier. It was becoming a habit. Why did he not simply speak to her?

Emmett Wood was never silent. Always the hiss of wind through the leaves, the knock and creak of branches, birdsong, the huh-huh of a 2-man saw, the whir of a bodger's lathe. Any new sound was easy for the woodlanders to pick up, and Edmund had made enough noise for three men that day. Those outside Emmett Wood thought of the inhabitants as fae folk and somewhat slow of wit. Strange in their dress and manners. Betony slipped on her soft leather shoes and twirled her skirts. She would be fae.

Edmund saw her stand. Was she looking at him? He felt her eyes, yet she could not possibly see from that distance. When he was certain her back was towards him, he stood and cautiously climbed over the long moss-smothered root. Her song had changed. This new song was lighter, quicker, full of trills and repeats. A dance through the crisp air that he could not ignore. He started after her. He kept the same distance at first, from behind tree to behind holly bush, until he was convinced that each time he paused, she did also. She was waiting for him, leading him to her.

Betony stopped for a moment where two paths crossed on the woodland floor. A moment later, Edmund's cacophony also stopped. Time to see how far he would follow. She chose a path, and skipped along waving her pale shawl above her head as her feet pattered across beech masts and year-before's leaves. She slowed so that he gained, then spun onwards.

Edmund felt more exposed following a path and kept stepping off to one side or the other when a shrub provided cover. Yet he dare not wait there long and lose sight of her altogether. He was breathing hard now, unused to more than walking pace. For a moment he thought she had disappeared. The path ran on ahead of him yet she was nowhere to be seen along it. Then to the east, though Edmund had lost all sense of direction now, her song trickled through the trees to him again. He leaped a fallen trunk and now paying no mind to the noise, crashed through the wood after his quarry.

Yes, he was running now. She would have to make haste. The ground began to fall away, the air grew thick and damp. She was confident that she would out-pace him, but she needed the advantage if she were to enjoy the end. She knew every tree, every clearing and every hollow. The steep drop to the river did not surprise her; she jumped to avoid the muddy ground at the bottom and bounded to the north. Three steps on the pebble shore so as not to disturb the reeds, then back onto the bank and up, clinging to an ivy ladder, until perched on a stump, knees drawn up and shawl wrapped around her, she waited.

Edmund had no knowledge of the drop. He came at speed from the trees into the comparative brightness of the riverbank and had no time to adjust. Down he tumbled, into the mud where the river Wynn twice daily crept. On hands and knees, face splattered and red, he swore. Only then did he realise the song had ended. He looked up, out across the river with its grey slick of clouds reflected. Now the hiss was through the reeds and a single curlew called from the fields on the opposite bank. She had vanished.

He got to his feet, stepping onto an old trunk that crumbled but gave him a platform from the mud. His only route was to climb back up the steep bank, for he was not a man for swimming. She had known, he admitted. His shame flickered into anger. She had known and she was responsible for his fall. He would not follow again; he would not forget.

CANDLEMAS IN EMMETT

THE FIRE HAD EXHAUSTED its first rage of flame and settled into glowing embers tinged with blue and green. Sparks rose occasionally as a branch was consumed, or a potato extracted with a long stick into waiting felted mittens. The woodlanders of Emmett sat as close to the fire as they dared; their faces red and smiling, their backs cold despite coats and blankets around their shoulders. Anticipation was growing. The age-old sequence of events on Candlemas night was known to all: bless the trees, light the fire, eat and drink, watch the Mummers' play, then disappear into the night.

They had gathered as the sun began to set; like beetles emerging from the woodland in shades of bark and moss. Some newcomers to the village of Emmett Green had raised concerns about the pagan traditions, petitioning the vicar at the end of several Sunday services. He had tried to reassure them in his generous and somewhat bewildered way, that the people of the woods would do no harm. He pointed to the carved faces surrounded by leaves, berries and nuts in the ceiling of the church and on the pew ends. The two outlooks had co-existed peacefully for centuries. Still, the newcomers watched with muttered distaste as the woodlanders assembled. Their dark clothes and dark skins, their deep sonorous voices and their watchful dark eyes held knowledge and community that the newcomers perceived as hostile and wild.

In nineteen twenty-seven, the tree blessing was led by Vernon Trow. It was not his first year of doing so. Considered one of the elder woodlanders, Vernon Trow was approaching his sixtieth year and had led the tree blessing every two or three years since he and his bride Avens had taken the wooden house two miles into the woods to the east of Emmett Green. Born just three miles north, to parents whose ancestors had never strayed beyond Wynn Vale, Vernon Trow was a true woodsman and held the respect of his community.

Though the woodlanders of Emmett looked on the trees as their own, in reality the two thousand and twenty-three acres of broadleaf and coppice belonged almost exclusively to the Marchett Estate. Bordered to the east by the river Wynn, there were two main settlements in the woodland: the growing village of Emmett Green in the south-east and the much smaller collection of cottages known as Little Birch in the north-west. There was also a small pocket of industry around Emmett Warf, consisting of the sawmills, owned by the Marchett Estate, and the paper mill which sat further upstream on the tributary and was owned by the Kemp family.

The bargees had long been responsible for taking the paper from the mill down to the town of Wynnham, or along the canal to Derring in the west. They were also the main source of news for the woodlanders, and though the trade was now much diminished, the Patrin and Greenway families still ran two barges up and down the waterway, carrying people, livestock or anything else too difficult to take the longer route by road.

The woodlanders did not live in the stone and brick houses that huddled together in those communities. It had been settled over a century before that they could live rent-free in the woodland as long as no permanent structures were built. They favoured small two- or three-room timber homes, built over several days from trees selected explicitly for that purpose. These cabins were situated in small groves, families usually staying in their own grove and building more small cabins to accommodate the generations. A few woodlanders preferred small caravans, similar to those used by the showmen and their families who visited the Vale two or three times a year. These were generally unpainted, and often used by young men before taking a wife and building their own cabin.

Paths wound between the groves, trodden by the wooden-soled work shoes of the woodlanders and the shod hooves of their horses. While the sawmills at Emmett Basin were mechanised and modern, the woodlanders used their own Percheron horses to haul the timber. These horses, mostly grey or dappled black, were kept in paddocks on the edges of the wood and brought to the wood to work. The horsemen could trace the bloodlines back to western France some two-hundred years earlier. New mares were occasionally brought up-river, but foals and yearlings were rarely sold outside of Wynn Vale.

The relationship between the woodlanders and the horsemen was symbiotic. Each woodland family would have a close bond with one who bred horses and managed farmland, thus maintaining a regular source of food for one and fire, fencing and tools for the other. Each was free to trade with anyone else they chose, but the kinship between the two families created strong ties and provided opportunities for managing the environment and the welfare of all in a sustainable way. The caravans that the woodlanders favoured were also useful when they worked with the farmers. They would be pulled out to the fields by the horses and enabled the woodlanders to work longer hours, eliminating the walk to and from the groves each day. The people of the woods disliked brick buildings; they found them claustrophobic and cold.

The Marchett Estate largely ignored the people of Emmett woods. It took resources from the land as they were needed, but only interfered with the lives of the woodlanders when it came to settling disputes and keeping the peace. A true outbreak of hostility had not occurred for many years, not since Vernon Trow was a young boy. The poor harvest of 1872 had caused some tensions to overflow and the Estate's then owner came down hard on poachers. Tempers flared and the bailiffs fought with a contingent of woodlanders who tried to petition the Estate for alms.

That was now in the distant past. Vernon Trow had seen several Estate owners come and go since then. The current incumbent, Thomas Broadridge, enjoyed riding to hounds with his young wife and hosting weekend parties. His Bailiff, Edmund Prentice, lived in one of the gatehouses on the eastern approach to Marchett House and dealt with all of the Estate business as Thomas Broadridge's representative. Vernon Trow did not think highly of Prentice; the Bailiff's aloofness and sneering looks were at odds with the ways of the woodlanders. Vernon sensed a hostility from Edmund Prentice that he had never been able to fully understand, although he had long had his suspicions.

So it was that in the late afternoon on the second day of February nineteen twenty-seven, Vernon Trow was surprised to see Edmund Prentice on the edge of the little group of newcomers to Emmett Green who were observing the woodlanders emerging from the trees. The Bailiff would usually have kept away from the woodlander's festivals. Vernon nodded an acknowledgement to the vicar and continued along the lane to the wide sward of grass that marked the centre of the village. There were already some fifty woodlanders waiting there. They talked in low voices and carried jugs of milk and hunks of stale bread which the children knew were not for them. Slowly their numbers grew until Vernon Trow, his granddaughter Melody at his side, raised his walking staff high into the air.

"Woodlanders of Emmett! It is time to drive the Lord of Winter from the trees and call back Frith the Summer King. Who will join me?"

Almost two hundred voices answered, "We will!"

If the newcomers were expecting a show there on the green, they were disappointed. The crowd moved off, following Vernon Trow back along the lane, then taking a left turn up a track between two houses and melting into the wood. As each crossed the perceived threshold of the trees, they took up the song that had been threaded through their collective memories. Drums and bells accompanied the singers of the Candlemas Song.

Dark the nights have been so long,
Chill the souls of men since born,
Out of snow and frosty air,
The Winter Lord on branches bare.
Wake Emmett wake!
Quiet have the days become
Misty cold at toil and home.

Stores laid down are now depleted
Fires low and ills defeated.
Wake Emmett wake!
Now the time has come again,
Shoots to bring from field and lane,
Buds to open, leaf and fern
Creatures wake and birds return.
Wake Emmett wake!
Hear us, Lord of Winter white
Take your blankets out of sight.
Hear us as we walk and sing,
Welcome Frith the Summer King!
Wake Emmett wake!

Around and around they sang as they walked, stopping here and there at a tree that Vernon Trow had selected over the previous week. An oak, an ash, a beech and a holly, a birch, an elm and finally a hazel coppice near to his cabin. At each, the libations of bread and milk would be left on the tree's roots or pushed onto the naked branches. The drums and bells would be beaten rapidly before taking up the rhythm of the Candlemas Song again.

The clearing where Vernon Trow's cabin sat was wide, surrounded on three sides by coppiced hazels and on the fourth, a patch of brambles and nettles which gave way to a stand of straight birches. There he made charcoal, and wove sturdy hurdles out of the hazel and ash trees. He was acknowledged as one of the best hurdle makers in Emmett, and his granddaughter Melody had learned all he could teach her. They worked together; it made no difference that Melody was a girl, she could chop and split the slender boughs and pack the charcoal pits as well as any boy. She also knew how to lay a hedge so that it quickly became a solid barrier to large livestock, and from the women of Emmett she learned as much about the nourishing or poisonous vegetation around her as every other child of the wood.

The Candlemas bonfire had been built with sticks and off-cuts from across the woodland. It was soon blazing within a circle of large cut logs and stumps which were used as seats and tables. Food and drink were brought from each home and shared with the community of woodlanders. There were also a handful of others present from across the Vale; those who had moved away for one reason or another or who traded regularly with people of Emmett. The last of the bargees who worked the river Wynn were welcomed, as were the men from Wynnlea who worked in the sawmills at Emmett Warf. Sylvester Patrin's barge was tied up at Emmett Warf and he and his son Bartolomy, and his nephew Malachai Greenway sat with Sylvester's relatives smoking their long clay pipes and sharing stories.

Another who was not of the wood but who sat down to share the food and would later watch the entertainment was Holden Prentice. Son of the Bailiff, he held the position of gamekeeper on the Marchett Estate, under the eye of the more senior game-keeper Johnson Briar. Holden Prentice had a strained relation-ship with his surroundings; not high enough in status to attend the Estate parties as a guest, yet considerably higher than the majority of woodlanders and many of the newcomers to the villages. When Johnson Briar's eyes were not directly on him, Holden took on an air of superior importance and revelled in catching the woodlanders in misdemeanours, bringing them to the attention of his father who metered swift justice.

One or two of the young woodsmen, while not calling Holden friend, chose to spend their free time with him. They drank in the King's Oak inn at Emmett Green, and roamed the countryside taking what food and firewood they desired. Holden was generous with his money, when it suited him to be so.

He sat to one side of the bonfire, with his view of Melody Trow unobstructed. Holden was careful not to make his observation of the girl noticeable. He laughed with his companions at their jokes and toasted the Winter Lord and Summer King in equal measure. Everyone took furtive glances into the dark of the trees once the feasting began to wane, hoping to be the first to see the Mummers.

They were the last of their line. A collection of men and women who had once been a band twenty-strong and travelled in caravans with the showmen, they now numbered six and had broken away from the showmen's route to stay in the Vale all year round. The Mummers appeared at each festival, playing out ancient stories of dragons, knights and maidens, harsh lords and gentle queens. Their costumes were bright and colourful; sometimes they wore masks and other times would paint their own faces. Between the festivals they worked the land as labourers for hire.

A shout went up from the far side of the bonfire.

"Mummers! Mummers!"

Then a hush fell upon the woodlanders and they watched to see the first of the costumes which would hint at the play they were about to enjoy. It was slowly revealed to them: one of the players dressed from head to toe in a costume of green rags, sewn like leaves onto a long smock and hood. The player's face was painted black with his eyes enlarged. The children present shrank behind their parents and nervous giggles came from the young women. The Woodwose tale was a well-known one. In Crossley, across the eastern Vale, the Morris Men had a similar costume that was used in the spring, and in a small fishing community along the coast near the border with Devon, yet another version made an appearance on May Day, dancing around the streets goaded by the young men and attempting to grasp an unsuspecting maiden.

In that night's play, a knight and a woodsman were to fight the Woodwose, to protect a fair maiden and win her hand. Naturally the knight was loud and brash, and the woodsman strong and kind. Allegiances in the audience swayed between the characters, with boos and cheers and gasps and finally applause as the Woodwose was tamed and the woodsman won the heart of the maiden.

This was the signal for parents to take their young children home to their beds, for the Mummers to join the elder woodlanders for food and drink and tale-telling, and for others to melt into the trees and spend the night away from the eyes of their guardians.

MISCHIEF

VERNON TROW WAS NOT worried that Melody had wandered off into the wood while he had been talking to the Mummers. Melody was seventeen and knew the paths between the groves better than many of the woodlanders. There would be lanterns around the wood that night, placed where paths crossed or to show hazards like unexpected dips or pits in the ground. Melody would make her own way home when she was ready.

Vernon climbed into his bed and despite the chill February night, he kept his arms outside the covers, his hands both behind his head. He looked up at the familiar pattern of the woodgrain above his head and thought back to the days when he and his young bride, Avens Fernley, were the only ones living in the cabin. Then Melody's mother had been born. If Vernon had thought Avens to be a beauty – and he had, along with many other woodsmen – then Melody's mother was enchanting. They had named her Betony. Her hair grew long in black waves down her back, her eyes were the brown of winter beech leaves, and she was wild.

Betony Trow never stayed where she was left from the moment she could roll around. As soon as she could walk, she ignored the calls of her parents who had to chase after her if their backs were turned for just a moment. They tried sitting Betony in a highchair, but she climbed out. They tried using leather straps to keep her safe, but she wriggled out of them. Betony walked and climbed and had no fear. She learned quickly which plants stung or snagged her skin, and was often found near the working horses, or out on the edge of the wood where the bee hives stood in a pasture of clover.

Vernon had hoped for a son. Once he had recovered from the disappointment of a daughter, and resigned himself to having no more children as Betony took up all of Avens' time and attention, he hoped that he might teach Betony a worthy skill. Betony was not interested. What Betony wanted was to sing. She would wander into the trees and find a comfortable spot, then make up tunes and lyrics that spoke of the birds and animals of the woods. As she grew, Betony's songs grew with her to encompass the people she knew and the seasons, the ways of the woodlanders and their festivals.

It had been a natural progression for Betony to join the Mummers. She was not a great actress, but she could sing and by the age of fourteen she also had a small harp that she played to accompany her voice. Vernon had fashioned the harp frame, and had the strings made from the intestine of a goat. It had been a present for Betony's thirteenth birthday; he recalled the way she had tentatively stroked the strings, almost afraid to touch the harp at first. Avens had shown her how to pluck each one to make a different note, and then how to use all of her fingers to produce trills and chords. Betony had carried the harp off into the wood and perfected her technique. Two years later, she was ready to join the Mummers and they took her with them the next time they left Emmett.

When Betony returned to Emmett with the Mummers, she was pregnant with Melody though she did not tell Vernon or Avens and they did not guess. It was only when she returned on her own four months later, no longer able to keep her secret, that Betony asked to stay and have the baby in the cabin. Vernon and Avens hoped the baby would be the making of Betony. They hoped that she would settle down, and perhaps find a man of the woods who would take her and the child into his own cabin. It was not unusual for a young woman to have had one or more children before a public commitment to one man was declared. Sometimes it would be with the child or children's father and sometimes not.

But Betony was wild. She quickly grew tired of being depended on by the infant Melody. Betony did not like encumbrances, and would at any opportunity slip out into the wood leaving Avens to see to Melody. It came as no surprise to Vernon when the Mummers next played to the woodlanders that Betony once more convinced them to take her with them. Avens refused to let Betony take Melody with her. In truth, Betony did not argue much beyond a token protest. Melody had seen her mother only three times since that day and not at all since she was seven years old.

Vernon rolled over and pulled the goose-down quilt and blankets up over his shoulder. Avens had died when Melody was seven. Vernon missed her every day and dreamed of her still most nights. She had been his only love, there would never be another that touched his heart as Avens had. Whoever Melody's father was, he had tempered her mother's genetic influence; Melody had inherited Avens's quiet industriousness and Vernon's skill with the wood. He loved his granddaughter as his own child, though there was a much smaller place in his heart now for Betony.

The last that Vernon had heard, Betony was living in Audling, the county town of Wynn Vale. She was no longer with the Mummers but had developed an act with her harp and was singing in one of the playhouses. That had been some years ago. Vernon wondered if Betony were still there, or if she had moved on, even out of the Vale. As he lay in his bed, Vernon heard voices outside the cabin and recognised Melody's quiet laugh. He allowed his body to relax and closed his eyes.

The only way Melody Trow resembled her mother Betony, was in the way her hair fell in waves down her back. Melody's hair was auburn, shot through with golden threads that glowed in the sunlight. Her pale skin, much paler than the woodlanders', was freckled across her nose and shoulders, and her slender fingers were much stronger than many would suspect of such a quiet girl. Despite her name, music did not feature in Melody's life beyond the birdsong of the woods. Her interests were in the plants she had grown up tending, their properties for healing or causing harm, the birds and animals of the woods, and the small collection of old coins and broken utensils that she had found over the years beneath the leaf litter of the woodland. These she kept in a small wooden box at the foot of her bed.

That Candlemas night, Melody had walked away from the bonfire with her friends, to sit and talk and drink the sloe gin that every cabin made each summer. Melody and her friend Cicely, and two young men of a similar age had gone only a short distance into the trees, and had talked quietly while listening to the familiar calls and laughter coming from other groups and couples that evening. They made a second, much smaller fire, as the night was frosty. All woodlanders respected fire; there were small, cleared patches of the wood floor dotted here and there, surrounded with stones and with wooden pails nearby full of water or soil to be used when the fire was no longer needed.

As the sloe gin went down, the four friends were joined by Holden Prentice. He had taken his time to reach the small group, hoping to find Melody in good cheer from the gin. She had not drunk as much as he expected, but she was tired and after a while announced to her friends that she was going home. Holden Prentice said he would walk with her, his home at the gatehouse being along the same path. Melody was not flattered as Holden supposed she might be. Yet she was also not displeased to be accompanied. Melody had a trusting nature despite her mother's abandonment and began each day by seeing the good in everyone she met.

The large bonfire had been allowed to die low, and no other woodlanders were around its edges. The last of them had pushed the remaining half-burned branches into the centre and poured water around the outside before they had left.

"Well, thank you much for your escort, Holden."

"No need to hurry inside yet. I thought we could sit for a while."

"The frost is settling; I need my bed."

Holden moved between Melody and the cabin, "Stay for a while, no one will miss you."

Melody tried to step around him, "Really, Holden, I am going in."

He caught her arm and held it firm, "At least a kiss good night then."

"Don't be silly," Melody frowned.

"Of course, if you want more than…"

Holden pulled her towards him, catching Melody off balance. As they tumbled to the ground Melody gave a shriek. Instinctively Holden drew his hand back and slapped her face.

"They all said your mother liked it rough." He hissed at Melody as he struggled to kneel over her wriggling legs on the soft leaf litter. The damp soaked into his trousers, and through Melody's dress. She was fighting now, the realisation of possible outcomes having fired her temper.

"Get off me! Get off! You're mad if you think I'm interested in you!"

The cabin door opened and Vernon stood in his nightshirt and boots, holding his billhook by his side.

"Melody! Come in now," he called.

"Say any of this and there'll be trouble for you and the old man." Holden breathed into Melody's face, then began to get up.

Melody saw her chance and kicked out at Holden, catching him behind his knee. His leg gave way and he crumpled with a yell to the ground. Melody got to her feet but did not see Holden reaching for her ankle. In a moment they were both on the woodland floor again, fighting like badger cubs.

Vernon Trow came down the cabin steps and rounded the bonfire. The two writhing bodies before him locked in combat were too close and fast for the billhook to be any use. Vernon tossed it back towards the cabin and reached with both hands to pull the young people apart. Melody he managed to almost throw to his right as she had at the same moment let go of Holden's neck to ready a punch. This gave Holden the opportunity to kick himself backwards through the leaves and mud, and roll to his feet. His neck was red, his face scratched, and he knew he would have bruises in the morning.

"She's no more than a wildcat! You should keep her chained, old man." Holden wiped his bloodied nose on the back of his torn cuff.

Vernon Trow said nothing. His bones were old and he no more wished to fight with the young Holden than walk through the centre of the bonfire as she shortest route back to his bed. Yet he clenched his hands into fists, just in case.

"You woodlanders, all the same as each other," Holden spat. "Touched, the lot of you! In the head!" He tapped his temple and sneered. "There's better maids in Derring. She," he pointed to Melody, "should think herself lucky I even walked with her!"

Holden turned to skirt the bonfire and make his way home. Melody ran at him, but Vernon was quick enough to catch her in his arms and hold her fast.

"You're the animal, Holden Prentice!" she shouted.

Vernon waited until Melody stopped struggling, just as he had when she was small and had wanted to follow her mother. Back then she had dissolved into tears. Now she simply looked down at her torn dress and shook her head slowly. Pieces of leaf fell from her hair, where twigs remained.

"I should have known he wanted more than just to see me home, Granfer."

"Maybe, maybe not. It does no good to always think the worst of people. Come on in, it's long past bedtime."

Vernon Trow waited for Melody to walk in front of him around the bonfire, its bones black and grey and the flames now blue in the frosty air. He picked up his billhook, gave a final glance at the bonfire and followed Melody into the cabin. Blue flames meant mischief to the woodlanders. Vernon Trow was unsettled and slept poorly.

Melody also had a fretful night. Holden Prentice's sneer loomed at her as she slipped into dreams, and she woke two or three times with a jerk as her sleeping body fought him off again and again. Though trusting, Melody was not naïve. She understood the ways of men and women and knew one day she would become a wife. The women of Emmett were strong and intelligent, despite the assumptions of those outside the woods, yet some genetic quirk meant there were far fewer girls born there than boys.

Across the Vale, this imbalance resolved itself, helped in more recent times by the Great War. The families spread and mixed, which also provided a bed and a meal if one were to find oneself away from home for the night. In each town and many villages the same surnames could be found on headstones in the churchyards, above the doors of shops and public houses, and in the school registers. Some names, however, were synonymous with their original location. The Trows had always lived in Emmett, the Burfords in Wynnfallow, the Falconers in Crossley and so on.

When Melody finally fell asleep that Candlemas night, she dreamed of the summer, of bees and horses in the pasture and the warm sun on her skin.

THE SHAME

"HOLDEN, WHAT IS THAT mark on your neck?" Amelia Prentice squinted at her son across the breakfast table in the gate house.

Holden too had had a sleepless night. He was used to getting his way, and being matched in a fight by a girl – a girl from the woods – was more than his pride could tolerate. The small hours of February third had given him time to develop a plan. He had deliberately left off his silk stock that morning in the hope that his mother might notice the red scratches.

"It's nothing, Mother." He replied with a sigh which he knew would provoke further questions.

Edmund Prentice poured himself more tea from the pot. He too had noticed his son's lack of attire and the graze on the side of his face which was currently furthest from Amelia's sight and in shade from the morning sun.

"Nonsense, it is surely something. Come now Holden, you promised no more fights." Amelia's voice was thin and whiney.

"Were you in the woods last night?" Edmund asked.

"I was, and ... it really was nothing. A misunderstanding of sorts. I tried to avoid her, but she followed me around all evening like a lost lamb. Then suddenly we were alone, and I am sorry to say she became rather suggestive towards me. I do not wish to repeat her exact words, Mother, please don't ask. I rebuffed her, naturally, and she became violent. It was all I could do to restrain her. Such wild passions those wood folk have, particularly when the gin flows in their veins. She is clearly too headstrong for her old grandfather to handle now." Holden glanced across at his father.

"You should not mingle with the woodlanders, I have told you many times before." Amelia reached out and patted her son's hand in sympathy. "One day you will be head gamekeeper here, or on another estate, and they will do you no favours."

"Yes, Mother."

When Amelia had excused herself from the table, Edmund once more dabbed his mouth with the napkin.

"Vernon Trow's granddaughter?"

"It was nothing, Father."

A reason to remove one of the woodlanders and claw back a portion of the wood for the Estate's own use was always of interest to Edmund Prentice, despite his employer's ambivalence. There had been a time when he might have asked Betony Trow to a dance, yet she was never interested in anyone other than herself and her own fantasy world. He could hear her laughing at him even now.

Edmund stared out of the window at the parkland beyond the drive as he remembered Betony's singing voice through the trees. Then he turned to his son.

"The Estate will not tolerate such wanton behaviour. Finish your meal."

An hour later, father and son strode through the trees following the well-worn path to Vernon Trow's grove. The frost had given way to a cold stinging rain which the naked trees could not prevent falling on the men as they walked in silence. The morning was dark; February was not a favoured month in the Vale, being too wet, too cold and lacking in daylight.

Vernon and Melody had finished their breakfast early and were engaged in spoon carving in the covered lean-to at the side of the cabin. Making such small utensils during the winter months was common in Emmett; the wood shavings collected and sold to the paper mill to supplement the families' income. The Trows used cherry wood for their spoons, and had their own distinctive style with a slightly wider handle piece topped with a carved cherry. They worked in companionable silence, listening to the breeze through the black branches above them and the crackle of the small fire in the brazier.

Edmund Prentice rounded the cabin and stood a little way from the lean-to. From his pocket he drew a folded sheet of paper.

"Vernon Trow!"

Vernon looked up from his work, knife in hand. The last time he had seen Edmund Prentice in the groves, he had been evicting a family whose dog had worried some Estate sheep. Vernon's brow furrowed. He stood up slowly and ducked to avoid hitting his head on the lean-to's entrance. Melody also stopped her carving and glared at Holden Prentice standing just behind his father. She received a smirk in return.

"Edmund. You have business here."

Edmund Prentice noticed the knife still in Vernon's hand and took a step backwards, but held out the folded paper. He understood the habit of many people of Wynn Vale of asking questions as if they were statements of fact. He spoke with more confidence than he felt, though he was relieved to find Vernon and Melody alone.

"It has come to our attention that your granddaughter has been flaunting herself about Emmett."

Vernon Trow spat on the ground but did not answer. A cold stone of fear had lodged in his chest; he knew what was coming.

Edmund continued, "The Estate does not tolerate such behaviour. Particularly when it leads to violence." He sniffed, the rain had worked itself into his collar. "This is a notice to quit. You have until sunset tomorrow to leave this property."

"What! You can't make us leave!" Melody was on her feet and at Vernon's elbow in a second. Vernon raised his hand to quiet her.

"This is Estate land, Miss Trow."

"But we live here. He's the one flaunting himself!" She pointed at Holden.

Holden shook his head, hiding his smile for a moment, "You see what I mean, Father?"

"Sunset tomorrow. Anything left here will be destroyed." Edmund waited for Vernon to take the paper. His hand began to tremble no matter how hard he tried to steady it. They were the same height; the older man holding the other's gaze while slowly reaching to take the notice.

"I have agreements with the Estate for hedging 'til Midsummer."

"You forfeit those by her behaviour."

As soon as the paper left Edmund's hand, he turned and scurried back around the cabin and retraced his steps along the path. Holden gave the Trows a final scornful look and followed his father.

Vernon Trow looked up to the branches above his head, the freezing rain stinging his cheeks and brow. Melody took the sheet of paper from him and was furiously saying that they would not leave, that she would rouse the woodlanders and they would defend their home.

"Pack what you can carry," he said quietly. He could feel his heart fluttering in his chest and was trying to keep his breathing steady and constant.

"You're not going to fight this? You're just going to let them turn us out, Granfer?" Melody was staring at him, wide-eyed.

"We live here under the grace of the Estate. How would you have me fight that?" He gestured to the paper in Melody's hand.

"Raise the woodlanders! Go to Thomas Broadridge and tell him there has been a mistake. He has to listen!"

Vernon shook his head slowly. "He does not have to listen. That's what he keeps Prentice in the gatehouse for."

They stood, Vernon out in the rain and Melody in the doorway of the lean-to, for a long moment looking at each other. Both wanting the other to understand. Melody was the first to drop her gaze. She knew the tone of voice Vernon was using, his quiet solidity when he was right and no argument could be had.

"But this is our home..." Melody's voice broke.

"For one more night."

Melody thrust the paper at her grandfather and stormed off across the grove and into the trees. He did not call after her.

Vernon Trow put the paper into his waistcoat pocket and went back under the lean-to roof out of the rain. He sat down heavily on his wooden stool and looked at the litter of shavings on the floor and Melody's abandoned half-worked spoon and knife. A box of finished spoons sat between them; he would need to sell those quickly. Vernon's mind was trying to overcome the cold sick feeling in his stomach so that he could plan what to do and where to go. The shame of being evicted would lay heavy on the name of Trow, more so than anything his wayward daughter may have done in the past.

Melody ploughed through the wood towards Cicely's family cabin. She had grasped a branch and was swatting away stray briars from the path with no regard for them springing back and grabbing at her skirt. Her hair was thoroughly dulled by the rain and she began to recognise that as soon as she stopped moving she would quickly become chilled. She could hear the sound of axes chopping at a trunk in the distance. A few minutes later, Cicely's cabin came into view. Smoke curled upwards from the chimney; the women of the cabin were at home.

Inside the cabin, Melody warmed her hands around a mug of strong tea, a blanket draped across her shoulders. Cicely's grandmother watched her with cloudy eyes, her fingers rhythmically wrapping yarn around her four knitting needles.

"That Prentice was never a strong baby," she pronounced. "Bandy legs. His mother kept him indoors too much, scared of him mixing with the wood children."

"He's strong enough now. Thinks he owns the wood and everyone in it." Cicely muttered.

"I just don't understand why Granfer didn't tell him to sling his hook! He just stood there and said nothing."

Cicley's mother, Augustine Hurst, was also knitting with fine yarn on four needles. She sat in a rocking chair beside the little pot-bellied stove in the room the family used as a kitchen, dining room, sitting room and workroom. As she reached the end of the row, she let her hands and her work rest in her lap and looked across at Melody.

"Your Granfer is a proud man, Melody Trow. We all know the Estate could turn us out whenever they feel like it. What good would it do to argue? We are peaceful folk, you know that, and we respect authority. It's a great pity that Holden Prentice and his father are the ones with that authority, but that's just how things are. I've told Cicely many a time to keep away from him; that young man is nothing but trouble. No, your Granfer would never have argued with them."

"But we haven't done anything wrong!"

"From what you've said, you did one of the worst things possible to a man. You hurt his pride, made him feel small. A man like Holden Prentice wouldn't have taken that lightly."

"Hardly a man," Cicley's grandmother screwed up her nose.

"Yes, well, that's the difference between Holden Prentice and your Granfer. Vernon Trow can hold his head up and walk tall, whereas that Holden would have the whole of Emmett laughing at him if they knew he'd been beaten by a girl." Augustine glanced at Cicely, who was chuckling to herself. "And you'll not start that gossip either, my girl."

"No, Mother."

Melody finished her tea, but still cradled the mug. She was as familiar with Cicely's cabin as she was her own. Augustine and Avens had watched over the girls as they grew, allowing each woman some time to work, clean, and sometimes recover from illness. When Avens died, Melody spent more time at Cicely's cabin when Vernon was laying hedges around the Vale. She and Cicely were as close as sisters, despite Cicely having three sisters of her own and two brothers.

With Cicely's grandmother also living with the family, there was no room for Melody to stay with them. She knew it and did not even ask.

"Will you go to the Summerton farm, do you think?" Cicely asked quietly. It was the farm that the Trows had the longest association with; a seventy-acre tenant farm with mostly Friesian cattle.

Melody shrugged her shoulders and sighed. "It will be down to Granfer. I'd better get back to him and pack my things."

Vernon Trow had considered the Summerton farm, but knew they would be hard pressed to find room there. Families were still large in the Vale, and farms in winter had many mouths to feed. Vernon would also not want to bring more misfortune to the farm if Prentice and his son were not satisfied with the distance between them and the Trows. That weighed heavy on his mind. Any offer of accommodation within Emmett Wood could lead to further retribution. Times were hard and Vernon had to think of Melody's future as well as his own.

Vernon had begun to set aside the items he would take with him the next day. He would use his pack, which he often filled with overnight things when his work took him across the Vale in the spring. Though the Trows' cabin was sparsely furnished, they would need warm clothes, tools and what few keepsakes and memory-gifts they had accumulated over the years. He would not be able to take Avens' kitchenware. To anyone else it would have no value, but Vernon's hands began to tremble at the thought of parting with it all. That little flutter again in his chest made him sit down for a moment.

After gathering himself, Vernon moved across the cabin to the space where he slept. In a drawer underneath his bed, wrapped in a yellowing handkerchief, was a wooden hair comb. Avens had used it to keep her coils of light brown hair anchored and away from her eyes. It was cherry wood, and on the flat portion above the long teeth, a single circle of amber had been set. It glowed like honey as Vernon touched it gently, then he wrapped the handkerchief around it again and placed the parcel into his pack.

Their evening meal was eaten in the silence that had crept into the cabin during the day. Melody had brought back a smaller pack, borrowed from one of Cicely's brothers, to fill with her own chosen possessions. The realisation that Avens' kitchenware, along with the teapot and china cups she had so prized, would have to be left behind brought tears to Melody's eyes.

"Granfer," she asked as she handed him a mug of sweet tea, "where will we go tomorrow?"

Vernon Trow had made his decision, though he did not know how it would unfold.

"We will go to your mother."

Melody looked across at him sharply. "Mother? In Audling? Can't we stay in Emmett?"

"I think you know, Prentice does not just want this cabin and the land. If we tried to stay here, he would be forever watching and making more trouble – for us and for anyone we stopped with. We have to move away, out of his reach. It's about time your mother played her part in this family."

"Do you even know where Mother is? How could we find her?"

"I believe she will be near a playhouse. I don't think she will be so hard to find."

In truth, Vernon Trow had no idea whether Betony was still in Audling or if she had followed the Mummers elsewhere, or even if she was still alive. What he did know was he and Melody had no other option.

They agreed that they would not wait until sun-down to leave the cabin the next day. Travelling at night in the winter was an unnecessary hardship. Vernon wanted to go down to Emmett Warf after breakfast and see if the bargees were about to take him and Meldoy upstream. He would say his goodbyes to the men at the sawmills and and ask that no retaliation be made in his name.

Melody went back with their travel plans to Cicely's cabin and Augustine organised Cicely and her sisters to carry as much from the Trow's cabin back to their own as they could. Avens' kitchenware would be taken care of, she assured Melody, and Vernon when he returned to find the procession of women and furniture passing back and forth along the grove paths. The bargees had not been at the warf; Vernon and Melody would have to take the road on foot.

It was perhaps a mark of Melody's unknown father that she showed her emotions far quicker than most woodlanders. She cried her goodbyes to Cicely and her sisters, and clung to Augustine for much longer than even the older woman was comfortable with. No one else came to see them off. It would have been considered bad-taste, revelling in the misfortune of others, for the woodlanders to gather for such an event. They respected Vernon Trow enough to not cause him to share his upset or distress.

The cabin was almost empty. There were no keys to hand back. Vernon and Melody slowly hefted their packs as the February sun briefly showed itself between heavy grey clouds. They lingered a moment longer, neither of them wanting to be the first to turn away. Melody slipped her hand into Vernon's and the left the grove together.

TWO BECOME ONE

THE ROAD FROM EMMETT Green to Audling passed through farm-land before sweeping north over the moorland. It forked just beyond Little Birch with a fingerpost declaring the distance to Derring was seventeen miles and the distance to Audling, twenty-three miles. Vernon and Melody had endured three heavy showers of hail by the time the sun dipped below a stand of beech trees on the western hillside. They had walked almost eighteen miles and were exhausted. Few vehicles had passed them that day; they had not expected to see many until they reached the main road between Derring and Audling which was still some twelve miles distant.

Vernon had hoped to see a barn or outbuilding that they could sleep in, away from the cold wind and rain. He had rarely ventured this side of Emmett, working mostly to the east of Wynn Vale and the productive farmland there, and had not realised the extent of the moorland. Very few people lived there, and those farms which existed had homes set back from the road along straight narrow lanes often a mile or more long. Ragged sheep wandered across the brown hills, leaving tufts of fleece on the low-growing gorse for birds and small rodents to gather in the spring.

A tributary of the river Wynn snaked its way down from the moor, and some industrious forefathers had built a stone bridge to cross it. The stream was low; the banks shallow with a fine silt beach at each curve. Vernon told Melody to wait with the packs while he investigated the path that led down from the road. A few minutes passed before he appeared again half-way up the path.

"Bring the packs down, we'll shelter here tonight."

"Is there a hut?" Melody's feet were blistered despite the two pairs of socks she wore.

"No, but under the arch is dry enough. There's tinder for a fire." He turned back towards the bridge as he took his pack from Melody, not wanting her to see the pain on his face that he was feeling in his shoulder and right arm.

They made camp under the bridge that evening with a small fire of wood that had been brought downstream and caught in a bend. They ate bread and cheese and drank weak tea, not wanting to use up too much of the provisions they had brought away from Emmett. They spoke little; there was little to say. The wind dropped, which they both knew would mean a frost. Melody walked a little way further than the bend in the stream and found a larger branch. She dragged it back to the bridge and with a couple of large stones and a tarpaulin from the bottom of Vernon's pack, they fashioned a windbreak screen so that they were protected on two sides from the worst of the weather.

Melody dreamed in the short snatches of sleep she had that night. The first dream was of the Mummers and the Woodwose, but instead of being tamed by the knight or the woodsman, it carried off the maiden who kicked and screamed and reached out to Melody pleading with her to intervene. Melody woke, turned over and tried to find a comfortable position in the hollow she had created.

The second dream was of the stream; a low barge was floating in the centre of the waterway. Melody and Vernon climbed aboard, but could not make the barge move downstream towards the river Wynn. Then the water began to rise, far higher and faster than she had ever known until the arches of the bridge were full. The barge rose on the tide and finally shot off downstream at such a pace that Vernon was thrown backwards from it and Melody screamed as his head disappeared below the swirling torrent.

Melody woke with a start, unsure whether she had actually shouted out in her sleep. She lay still for a while, listening to the sound of the running water. Her hood was pulled up over her head but she could feel the cold on her face. She had put on almost all of the clothing she owned and was under a felted blanket, her feet towards the now extinguished fire. Eventually she drifted off to sleep again and dreamed briefly of the bee hives on the Summerton's farm. Their humming was soothing and the next time Melody woke, there was a finger of pale sky on the horizon.

Vernon was still under his blanket. Melody went to relieve herself behind the tarpaulin, then gathered a handful of twigs and branches and set about relighting their fire. She filled the tin kettle from the edge of the stream and set it to boil. A robin landed nearby and cocked its head at Melody, as if wondering why humans would be out so early on such a cold morning. There was a plop as a water vole took to the stream on the far bank. Melody wondered if she should try wading into the water to try and catch a fish before they started off again. Then she shook her head at the absurdity of the idea; she would freeze in seconds with her bare feet in the icy water.

The kettle began to wobble as the water inside came to the boil.

"Granfer, I'm making tea." Melody said as she carefully lifted the kettle off the fire with a stout stick. Resting it on the ground, she looked over at where Vernon still lay. It was unusual for him to sleep much beyond five even on the dark winter mornings.

Melody stood up and looking down at Vernon, she knew something was wrong. He was too still. His back was towards her and she hesitantly stepped around his feet so that she could see his face. He looked as if he were still sleeping, his hands clasped up to his chest. Even in the half-light, Melody knew. Vernon's skin was grey.

She dropped to her knees beside him, leaning down until her face was almost level with Vernon's. She could see the stubble on his chin and the frost on his eyelashes. Melody gently stroked his cheek, her lip trembling and tears now falling. She leaned into him, her head against his, and wrapped her arm over his body. She lifted his head with her hands, and momentarily wondered at its weight, before gently lowering it to the sweater he had used as a pillow that night.

Melody sat, hugging her knees, the tea forgotten now. What should she do? Could she go back to the wood and find help to take Vernon home? But the wood was no longer their home, and if she left Vernon under the bridge, the river could rise and carry his body away or worse, the animals might begin to return him to the earth. Melody had no idea where the nearest farm or house might be. She began to rock side to side, sobbing now with the knowledge that she was utterly alone. The shame that she had refused to acknowledge the day before now weighed on her; this was her fault. The dawn grew almost imperceptibly from that slim finger until everything beyond the banks of the stream was revealed as frozen and white. The robin returned briefly, but finding no crumbs, did not linger.

Melody's sobs began to ease and her teeth started to chatter. She looked again at her grandfather, then crawled back to the fire and the kettle. She decided to forego the tea and drank a little hot water instead, using a drop more to wipe her face before refilling the kettle and placing it back on the fire with a few more sticks. Her life had been free of the need to make major decisions up to that point.

She sat beside Vernon for what felt like days but was a little more than an hour. Her mind repeated over and over, Granfer is gone and you are alone. Melody might have stayed there until she too perished from lack of food or water, so confused by grief and her sudden initiation into the world of adults and responsibilities, yet the sound of a horse's hooves on the road approaching the bridge roused her. She scrambled up the path and stood by the side of the bridge, waving her arms above her head.

Abbot Cranshaw had made an early start that morning, keen to be at the livestock market in Audling and look over the young rams before bidding began the following day. Dressed in his usual rough trousers and jacket, a blanket over his knees and a cap on his sandy hair, he looked no different to any other farm worker across the Vale. His horse was one of the treacle-brown moorland ponies, broken as a yearling and content now to pull the small cart that Abbot sat on at a trotting pace. They kept more modern machinery but Abbot preferred the cart and liked working the horses.

As Abbot approached the bridge, Melody's frantic appearance and arm waving caused the pony to shy. It tried to side-step in its harness and almost turned the cart into the ditch. Melody realised her error and ran to help calm the horse, talking quietly to it and blowing down her nose, nodding her head as she had been taught to do with the Percheron around Emmett. Eventually the pony's eyes lost their terror and it allowed itself to be led back into the middle of the road. Abbot had not moved from his seat while Melody attended the horse. Her appearance had surprised him as much as the animal; from his vantage point he was struck by the fearless way she approached the pony, her hair dishevelled and her movements hampered by the layers of clothing she wore. He would have taken her for a vagrant had she not been clearly a young woman.

"I'm sorry I frightened him, but I needed you to stop. It's my Granfer. He's under the bridge. He's ..." Melody couldn't bring herself to say the word.

"Under the bridge? Is he ill?"

Melody nodded her head, tears spilling down her cheeks again. Abbot looped the reins over the footboard and jumped down into the road.

"If you'll hold him, I'll go and take a look."

While Abbot was gone, Melody leaned against the pony and gave in to her tears again, clinging to its mane. The animal stood calmly, having decided that she was not about to do it any harm.

Abbot, meanwhile, approached the body of Vernon Trow with caution. He was aware of the ruse some beggars used to lure an unsuspecting traveller from the road to be robbed or worse. He had seen for himself the way some soldiers would pretend to be dead, then at the last minute rise up and fire point blank into the enemy.

"How are you, old man?"

When there was no reply, Abbot crouched down nearer to Vernon's head. Now Abbot could see the pallor of the skin and the lack of rise and fall of the chest. He knew a dead man when he saw one. He swore and sat back on his heels for a moment. This was not how he had imagined his day would begin.

Melody had composed herself again by the time Abbot climbed back up to the road. They looked at each other and Abbot shook his head. Melody nodded to signal her understanding.

"Where is your home?" Abbot asked, hands deep in his pockets despite his leather gloves.

Melody bit her lip. She looked back along the road she and Vernon had travelled the previous day, then met Abbot's eyes.

"We have no home."

Abbot frowned. "Well, we can't just leave him there." He looked at his watch, scratched his chin, and came to a decision. "I suppose the rams can wait. Will you be all right to wait here while I go back and fetch a couple of hands? I won't be long, perhaps an hour."

"You will come back though?"

"I will. You should rekindle the little fire you had down there and keep as warm as you can. Here, take this." He pulled the blanket off the cart seat and handed it to her. "Now I've got to come back," he smiled.

Melody's big eyes did not smile in return.

As the cart rumbled along the lane towards the farm, Abbot considered the strange girl under the bridge and the old man she had been travelling with. They had not looked down at heel as most vagrants he had encountered did. Her hands and face had been clean; she had not smelled noxious. The old man of course had the smell of death on him, but he too was clean shaven and his clothes and boots were in good repair. Abbot had seen much worse in the trenches.

As he reached the yard, he called out to the small group of labourers who had gathered to be given that day's work assignments. They certainly resembled vagrants far more, Abbot conceded, in their old clothes and worn boots, scarves tied around their necks. The farm kept seven men and three boys in employment, though in the winter months there were often days, sometimes weeks where no meaningful work could be found for them all. The boys were set to keeping the horses clean, fed and exercised, but it had not been unusual that year for the farm to pay its stipend to the men for no exchange of labour. It had been his father's decision years ago that his field workers would not become destitute because of the weather. Their pay was reduced, but not withheld completely. What, Abbot wondered, would his father have done that morning in his position?

"I need two men to come with me. A sorry task I'm afraid, there is an old man under Fenny Bridge who has died in the night. We're going to bring him back here."

The men glanced at each other. A sorry task, indeed; though none of them were strangers to death, none of them were eager to make its acquaintance again so soon. Eventually two men nodded and climbed aboard the cart. Abbot turned it in the yard and called over his shoulder for the remaining men to explain to Mr Roman that there would be no ram that week, but they would be in need of a coffin-sized box.

Roman Cranshaw was the eldest surviving son of Robert and Catherine Cranshaw. He and Abbot had returned from the Great War relatively unscathed physically, but their older brother David had been one of the many fallen at the Marne. Abbot had seen only nine months of battle; Roman had by some miracle survived almost four years. They returned to find their father close to death after suffering a series of strokes. The news of David's death had also laid heavy on Catherine Cranshaw, and with her husband so ill, she happily handed over the running of the farm to Roman. Three months later, Robert Cranshaw was dead and his surviving sons officially became the owners of South Weald farm.

Before the war, Roman and Abbot had never given a thought to running the farm. It had always been assumed that David would stay and take it on, while the two younger sons made their way in the world following their interests in mechanical engineering and law. Now as Roman joined the remaining men in the yard, the responsibility of keeping their tenants occupied was not improved by Abbot's good Samaritan behaviour.

"You two take the feed up to the sheep at Hillcrest. The rest of you can go back to the ditch clearing. Boys, one of you take the bicycle and go over to Doctor Mitchell and ask him to come out this afternoon. Then we'll have the end stable cleared and trestles set up ready to hold some boards. Whoever this man is, he'll have to wait for a coffin, I want the doctor to see him first."

With the hands dispatched, Roman went back into the house, annoyed that they would have to wait longer for a new ram to join their flock. The house itself was built in the late seventeen hundreds of local granite with two wings and a large central hallway. At times it had been partially covered with roses, then ivy, then wisteria. Now it was roses again, a yellow variety badly in need of pruning and training around the windows. Roman strode through the formal dining room to the morning room at the rear of the house. Its windows looked out across their farmland and it was where his mother spent most of her days.

Catherine glanced up at Roman as he entered the room. He knew there would be coffee on the low table near Catherine's chair, and poured himself a cup.

"It seems as if we shall need the undertaker's services. My brother has found a body down by Fenny bridge."

Catherine did not reply. She rarely spoke now, just sat waiting for the day she could join her husband. Roman had not expected a response, yet he continued as he often did, criticising Abbot or the hands, or both.

"Why he couldn't simply have kept going and then collected the body later, I have no idea. Idiot that he is, we'll have lost our chance to bid for that Devon Closewool ram that was in the sale catalogue. If we don't get one in soon, we'll have to arrange a stud ram and I really would prefer not to."

Roman stood at the window sipping his coffee, looking out across the fields. The rooks were disturbed on the edge of the woodland that formed the southern end of the farm. It lay in a valley between two steep hills currently studded with distant ewes and in its depths the source of the tributary that Melody and Vernon had camped beside could be found.

"We also need some new hurdles. I can't see how we can avoid buying those, the hands are simply not up to the job."

Melody had not wasted the time waiting for Abbot to return. She had coaxed the fire back to life, then dismantled the windbreak they had made the evening before. As she began to refold the tarpaulin, it occurred to her that some form of stretcher would be needed to carry Vernon up to the road. There was one long branch that had been used for the windbreak, and she quickly found a second of a similar length and girth. Using a piece of rope from Vernon's pack, she bound the two edges of the tarpaulin to one of the branches, then slid the second branch in between the folded sheet. With Vernon's body on top, it would serve them well.

A motor car rumbled over the bridge. For a moment Melody wondered if it might be Abbot returning, but the car continued towards Emmett. So Melody sat, cross-legged on the sandy bank of the stream, shoulders covered with the blanket, watching the flames flicker until she could hear the horse's hooves. When they came to a halt, she hoped it would be Abbot. Voices came down to her on the path at the side of the bridge, and then he was there in front of her.

"Did you make this?" Abbot pointed at the makeshift stretcher on the ground beside Vernon's body.

"I thought it would help."

Oh, it will. Well, come along you two, move the old man onto the tarp and get him safely up onto the cart." He waved his hand towards the body and gave the two men a look that invited no argument.

"Where will you take him?" Melody poured water over the small fire.

"Back to the farm. Beyond that I haven't given much thought. But you must come too; it's not safe for a young woman to be out on her own wandering the moor." Abbot spoke softly. He had not thought much how or where they would see Vernon buried; his thoughts had been more for the living, and for Melody in particular. He was curious about how she came to be under the bridge; where had she come from and why? Now was not the time to ask, he knew that. Instead, he held out his hand to help Melody to her feet, they picked up the packs and slowly they followed the two men as they cradled Vernon's body on the stretcher up to the cart.

A WOODEN HOME

MELODY HAD NEVER BEEN in a real bathtub before. In the cabin, they had used a galvanised tub occasionally, but more often simply washed themselves with a bowl of warm water. Now in the Cranshaw's bathroom, she tried not to move too quickly having already twice splashed water onto the floorboards.

A maid had come out to the cart after Abbot had sent one of the men to fetch her. She was a little older than Melody and reminded the girl of Cicely's older sister Tansy. The maid, Agnes, explained how the bath worked and left Melody to her ablutions with a pile of towels, saying she would return in half an hour and take Melody down to the kitchen for something to eat.

The soap smelled of honey. Melody wondered if it had been made on the farm. She lay back in the water until her head was fully under, then breathed out a stream of bubbles before surfacing again. Working the soap into her hair, Melody's mind slipped back to Vernon. How cold his head had been in her hands and against her cheek. Who would do the laying out? It dawned on Melody that she might have to. She could not stop the tears from falling again into the bath water. She was still crying when the maid returned.

"There now, don't take on so. This is a good place, they look after us all right. Let's get you dry and some food into you and things won't feel so bad." Her voice wasn't totally convincing, but Melody allowed herself to be wrapped in a large towel as she stepped out of the water and began to dry herself. The maid produced a hairbrush, placed it on the shelf below the mirror, and waited until Melody was dressed and ready.

"What do I call you?" Melody asked as she followed the maid down the stairs.

"Agnes. And you?"

"Melody Trow."

"That's a pretty name. Unusual." By unusual, Agnes meant strange; she suspected it was a gypsy name of some kind.

Melody decided not to elaborate.

They passed through a dark wood-panelled hallway on their way to the kitchen and heard raised voices behind a door.

"...Good heavens man, it's not our responsibility!" Roman shouted in exasperation.

Melody did not ask Agnes who it was they could hear; she understood instinctively that the topic of discussion was related to Vernon and herself. It seemed that she was causing trouble again.

The kitchen was typical of a small Georgian manor house. In the centre of the tiled floor stood a large wooden table, scrubbed almost white over the years. To one side was a large black range which had some eighty years before replaced the open fire pit and hand-cranked spit. A room off the kitchen served as a pantry with a marble cold shelf and hooks for meat, game and fish. Copper, iron and enamelled pots and pans crowded the shelves, with knives and other utensils of all shapes and sizes hung from individual hooks underneath. A second room was used as a small dining room for the house staff, and just beside the external door was a small washroom which had thoughtfully been divided into separate toilet and laundry area.

Standing at the kitchen table was a short woman, who Melody guessed might be around fifty years old. Her hair was dark grey; she wore glasses with small round lenses, attached to a chain around her neck. Her sleeves were rolled up and she was chopping a haunch of beef into small cubes. Without looking up, she addressed Melody.

"All clean now? Bless my soul, you did look a state when you came in! And when was the last time you had something to eat? Days, I expect. Agnes, give the maid some of that cheese and potato pie we had last night. That should keep her going until lunch is ready."

"Thank you much, but I'm not hungry." Melody watched the cook's knife slice through the flesh with ease and felt her stomach turn over. She had never liked to watch Vernon prepare the rabbits or fish he brought in for their evening meals. Vernon ... Melody swayed as if she might faint and Agnes grabbed at her in alarm.

"Here, sit down before you fall down. I think you're more hungry than you know."

Satisfied that Melody would not sink to the floor, Agnes took a plate and cut a portion of pie, bringing it back to the table with a fork.

"Just a little bit for now. Go on."

Melody sighed. She really didn't feel hungry, but it would be rude to refuse food. She picked up the fork and tested the pie crust. The shortcrust pastry was evenly golden and broke easily. As Melody lifted the fork to her mouth a door slammed back along the hallway causing all three women to pause. The cook raised an eyebrow, "Wonder which of the gentlemen that was."

"Mister Roman was shouting as we came by. They never seem to agree on anything these days."

"And who's to wonder? Neither of them should be here by rights. Oh, I don't mean they should have not come home, what I mean is neither of them thought they'd have to stay here and run the farm. It was always meant to be Mister David's and not for a good few years yet, either."

"Mister Abbot could leave, go and be a solicitor like he wanted." Agnes sat down in the chair next to Melody.

"Oh no, he'll not leave his mother. Like two peas in a pod those two, both as soft as a goose pillow and not much more sense now, either. Talking of peas, put a couple of pound of those dried ones in that bowl to soak for me if you've nothing else to do." The cook gestured towards an enamel bowl on the end of the table with the point of her knife. Then she looked at Melody for the first time since she had entered the kitchen.

"Where'd you say you were from again?"

Melody swallowed and looked directly back at the cook, knowing she had not told anyone in the house yet.

"Emmett."

Though Melody had seldom been beyond Emmett wood, she was aware that the woodlanders were regarded as strange by many others in Wynn Vale. In days gone by, stories of fairies and elves were told in the surrounding towns and villages, with mild threats that they might steal away naughty children. Few people not born in Emmett felt comfortable spending any length of time in the wood, with the exception of the bargees, which only made suspicions of mystery and misdeeds grow stronger.

The cook met Melody's gaze and held it, the tip of her knife resting on the larger piece of beef.

"And the man in yonder barn?"

"My Granfer."

The cook's eyebrow raised slightly.

The atmosphere in the kitchen grew thick. Melody felt as if all the air had been sucked out of her lungs. She wanted to cry again but held herself in check. Slowly putting down her fork, she pushed the plate away and stood up.

"I need to be outside," she said, turning towards the hallway.

"I expect you do. But not that way. Use the back door like the rest of us." The cook's knife now pointed towards the washroom.

Melody felt her cheeks burn but she turned with her head up and forbid her legs to run as she left the kitchen.

"What was all that about?" Agnes asked, setting the bowl of dried peas on the draining board and filling a jug with cold water.

"Emmett. Woodlanders. Strange folk with strange ways. I knew a girl from there once, away with the fairies most of the time, she was. What was her name now... something Moss... whatever, them's not to to be trusted."

"What, all of them? Surely not everyone is the same?" Agnes was a kindly girl from a hamlet along the lane towards the coast, who had worked as a maid at the farm for almost ten years. Always thinking the best of people, the cook regularly told her she was too gullible. Cook often wondered how the girl had avoided falling for the charms of one of the farm hands for so long, with promises of a cottage down near the village of Robey. The Cranshaws owned several small properties in Robey, and a handful scattered around the edges of their land, mostly in pairs and housing staff and hands who had long since become too old to work.

"Anyone who keeps the company of the river rats would likely steal the teeth from your mouth while you were sleeping. You mark my words, Agnes Brown, they are trouble. And is that poor soul really her grandfather? Where are her parents? Why were they sleeping under Fenny Bridge and not in one of those wood huts they build for themselves? Something funny going on there."

"Melody seems nice though. And if he is her grandfather she must be terribly upset that he's died. I think that's what Mister Roman and Mister Abbot were arguing about. What do you do with a dead body that doesn't belong to you?"

Melody shut the outer door behind her and gulped at the cold air. The sun was a watery smudge in the palest blue sky, more a mirage than a circle, and only a little above the ridge of the hills. The kitchen entrance to the house was through a small vegetable and herb garden, standing bare except for some forlorn stalks of brussels sprouts and the last of the leeks. In the far corner of the garden stood a large glasshouse, its white painted woodwork stark against the orange of the brick wall behind it. Next to the glasshouse an iron gate was slightly open. Melody wanted to see what was on the other side.

The gate was well-used and did not give off any metallic grinding squeal she half expected as she pushed it further open. Now she found herself in a more formal garden area with two terraced lawns separated by a wide flower bed of herbaceous perennials, their stumps and brown stalks left to over-winter for the insects. There were no gardens like this in Emmett. If the woodlanders cleared a patch of soil, they planted food crops. Flowers were considered a luxury and often a poisonous one if not thoroughly respected.

Melody crossed the first rectangle of grass to where stone steps covered in orange lichen led down to the second terrace. As she reached the bottom step, she glanced to her right and found Abbot sitting on a stone bench looking up at her. He had been poking a stick into the ground at his feet, tearing up the grass like a squirrel desperately searching for hazelnuts.

"Oh, I'm sorry, I'll go." Melody turned to climb the steps again, but Abbot held up his hand.

"Not, it's quite all right. Please … don't run away."

Melody stayed on the steps, unsure what to say or do. The woodlanders considered interrupting a person clearly on their own with their own thoughts to be disrespectful and would change their route through the trees if they saw someone ahead of them. Only if they were called out to or invited to join the person would they go nearer. Many would whistle or sing to themselves while they worked to show they could be approached.

Abbot Cranshaw noticed that Melody's hair had been washed and brushed out, and that her cheeks were a healthy rose colour despite her pale skin. He noticed her long fingers as they rested on the stone side of the steps, and he noticed the worried frown on her face.

"You can sit down, here. I didn't bite when we travelled in the cart, did I?" He indicated to the space beside him, enough room for Melody to sit down with a good eighteen inches between them.

Melody hesitated. Holden Prentice's change of mood still fresh in her mind, and the consequences it had had for her and for Vernon. Yet Abbot was right, they had sat together much closer on the cart on their journey back from the bridge. Slowly Melody descended the final two steps and sat gingerly on the furthest corner of the stone bench. Immediately she felt the cold work through her clothes, and tried to position herself so that as little of her thighs and bottom were in contact with the seat as possible. It gave her a tenseness that Abbot took for nervousness and unhappiness.

"Did Cook give you something to eat?"

"I'm not hungry, thank you much."

"Well, if you are later, be sure to ask her."

"What will happen to Granfer?" It was at the forefront of her mind, she had to know.

Abbot sighed and looked out across the terrace towards the valley. "We have to wait for the doctor to see him."

"No doctor can mend him now!"

"No, no of course, but a sudden death has to be handled in the correct way. Do you understand? It would be remis of us if foul play had occurred and the appropriate authorities were not informed. Not that we do think that, or course..." He let his voice tail off, unsure if Melody really did understand. Roman had pointed out that no one knew how Vernon Trow had died, and they could be harbouring a felon with Melody in their home. Abbot had brushed his brother's concerns aside; the girl was clearly distraught at losing her grandfather, it was their moral duty to help in any way they could given the circumstances. Roman has vehemently disagreed, as usual.

Melody didn't trust her voice to talk about Vernon. She followed Abbot's gaze towards the tree-tops in the valley with the rooks flapping and jumping in the branches.

"I want to go to those trees." She stood up and began walking across the grass.

Abbot watched for a moment. She was certainly a strange girl. If Roman was right, and of course he wasn't, but if he was then perhaps Melody should not be allowed to wander the farm unescorted. He got up from the bench and followed her, keeping a few feet behind.

There was no definite path to the trees. Melody walked in a straight line, aware by the sound of his footsteps through the longer grass that Abbot was following her. She noted that he had not tried to stop her, nor insisted on walking by her side. He was a strange man. He used a lot of words to say simple things.

The ground dipped unexpectedly then rose again, giving a wider view of the valley. The land on this side of Wynn Vale lay as if drawn in a child's picture book; the curves of the hills layering into the distance with the grey of the English Channel revealed between two low points to the south. In the spring many of the hills would be turned into chocolate folds of rich earth; in summer they would become golden with wheat and corn, or shades of green studded with the white sheep. Tucked into the base of one hill, a collection of buildings with chimney smoke lazily hanging over the roofs came into view. Robey shivered in its frost pocket; the houses huddled around the central church as if for warmth.

Melody paid the scenery no attention. The closer she drew to the tree line, the quicker her steps became, the faster her heart beat. Abbot did not match her stride. He could keep the girl in his sight here without hurrying. He did not believe that she would run away – sure if she were going to, she would have that morning while he returned to the farm to collect the hands. Was it only a few hours that he had known her?

There was no fence around the edge of the woodland. The ground had a stony track between the grass and the low shrubby growth which gave way to saplings and young beech trees. Melody ploughed through the undergrowth and reached out to the first of the trees in her path. She caressed the bark of each as she passed by, slowing now, breathing deeply. The further she went, the taller and broader the trees became. Here and there a holly in deep green or a grey ash, but the beech trees dominated and littered the woodland floor with their masts. The relief of being in a familiar surrounding brought up a fresh wave of sorrow for leaving her home behind. She sat on a long-fallen trunk and forgetting Abbot behind her, put her head in her hands and sobbed.

Abbot wanted to go to her, but stopped and leaned against a tree. He rarely came here now; as a child he would rampage through the woodland pretending to chase deer or Roundhead soldiers (the Cranshaws had long been staunch royalists) with his brothers. David had loved the woodland and had begun to manage the resources just before the War began. Abbot doubted if anyone had been there since.

The distant chimes of Robey church told him it was eleven o'clock. Abbot shivered. He should see if the doctor had arrived yet.

"Melody!"

She wanted to lay on the ground and never leave again. To feel the soft leaf litter swallow her whole, the worms and beetles helping to bury her.

"Melody, we should go back to the house. You have no jacket, come along now." Abbot took a couple of steps closer, but still well out of arms' reach.

She lay her hands on the gnarled bark as if to draw out the last substance of the tree's life into her own, spreading her fingers wide like fungal hyphae. Then she stood, realising she had no handkerchief to wipe her face. Abbot realised at the same moment and pulled his own from a pocket.

"Here, use this. Keep it, I have another." He offered it to her without moving any closer.

Melody looked up into his eyes and he saw the confusion and sorrow clearly. His mother had worn a similar look when the news of David's death had arrived.

"Come along now," he said again, much quieter this time.

She took the handkerchief and they moved off, this time with less distance between them, back to the edge of the woodland

and the track. As they emerged into the open air once more, Abbot pointed down towards the church.

"This leads down to Robey village, where most of the farm hands come up from each day. It's the nearest church." He turned and indicated they should walk in the opposite direction, "And this way leads around to the side of the farmyard past the house and into the lane to the main road. The land on both sides is ours."

Melody felt heavy and weary.

Wanting to fill the space between them, Abbot continued, "It will take a few days to sort everything out I imagine. You can stay in the house until your grandfather is laid to rest, we have several spare rooms, I will tell Agnes to make up a bed for you."

"We were going to Audling."

"Oh. Well, then I can take you in the cart. Do you have relatives there?"

It was innocently asked, but Melody was on her guard. She had not wanted to see Betony again, though that had been Vernon's decision and she would not argue with him. Melody felt no love for her absent mother. She doubted that she would even recognise her now, and surely they would have nothing in common. Better to say she now had no family at all – which could be true for all she knew.

Abbot noted the pause before Melody answered.

"No. It was just where we were going. Granfer wanted to go there."

"Had you been travelling a long time? Have you come far?"

The cook and Agnes knew she had come from Emmett, there would be no sense in claiming otherwise now.

"From Emmett."

"I know of it. My brother David spent some time visiting the Marchett Estate there when he was studying land management. Do you know it?"

Melody nodded.

The woodland had given way to more pasture bordered with hedges that needed laying. Melody was beginning to feel light-headed again, and stopped to lean on a field gate. She looked out across the rough field with its collection of ragged sheep. To the side of the field stood a shepherd's hut, of the old style with wheels to enable it to be moved wherever the sheep were stationed. Grass grew tall around the wheels; it obviously hadn't been used in several years.

"I don't think I should stay in your house. I'd rather sleep there." Melody pointed at the hut.

"I'd quite forgotten about that old thing! You'd be much warmer in the house... I'm not even sure if the roof is still water-tight. As we're here, we might as well take a look."

Melody let go of the gate as Abbot pushed it open.

"Your hedges won't keep the sheep in if they're not laid."

"Just one more job on a farm this size that one never seems to get round to! And I wouldn't know where to start if I'm completely honest. I expect my brother will get someone in to do them. Now, it shouldn't be locked, let's see if the door will open."

He gingerly climbed the wooden steps and pulled at the door handle. It opened surprisingly easily, almost knocking Abbot back down the steps. Melody couldn't quite stop a smile from fleeting across her face as Abbot swore, his face reddening with embarrassment. They went inside, carefully testing the floorboards in case they gave way with rot.

A raised sleeping platform on one side had two drawers in the base. Opposite the platform, a small black stove with a pipe that reached upwards through the roof was the only other adornment. A small window which spiders had woven a lace curtain across was set into the far end wall opposite the door. They could not see the sky through the roof, which had been covered with curved sheets of corrugated iron, now rusted to a rich brown.

"I suppose it wouldn't take much to get it cleaned out. But look here, are you truly sure you wouldn't prefer to stay in the house? With a bathroom and a proper bed?"

Melody looked around at the wooden walls. "I am sure. It's like home."

ORPHANS

THEY RETURNED TO THE house along the track in silence, the pale sun now covered by grey clouds in a grey sky. Melody's mind was still half on the state of the hedges, but as they neared the rear of the stables the feelings of sorrow and loss began to envelope her again. Abbot was considering his own feelings for the strange foundling by his side. She was attractive without being beautiful; she was articulate though naturally he recognised she was upset and not in the mood for polite yet pointless small talk. Yet there was something more about her that drew him, and made him want her to stay if not in the house, then on the farm for as long as possible.

The doctor had arrived in his car shortly after the panting boy had returned. Roman Cranshaw had offered Doctor Mitchell refreshments before accompanying him across the yard to the stables where Vernon Trow's body had been laid on top of several planks, stretched across the top of three trestles. They were getting ready to return to the house when Abbot and Melody entered.

" ... no, I shouldn't think an invasive examination will be necessary. I will inform the coroner, naturally, but I am sure this can all be cleared up without too much fuss."

"Doctor Mitchell," Abbot shook the older man's hand. "This is the man's granddaughter."

The doctor looked Melody up and down but did not offer his hand. Despite the bath she had taken, he recognised something of Emmett about her; something he had also recognised in the clothes still covering Vernon Trow's body.

He cleared his throat. "Young lady, your grandfather died of natural causes in my opinion. A combination of the extreme cold weather and probably some disorder of his heart. How old was he, do you know?"

"Fifty-nine."

"A good age for someone who lived an outdoor existence." He spoke as if something rotten lingered on his tongue. He turned back to Roman, who had also been looking Melody up and down. "You'll arrange the undertaker. I will see to everything else. Good day to you Mister Cranshaw, Mister Cranshaw."

Again, they shook hands and Roman ushered the doctor out into the grey daylight. Melody crossed the stable and gently pulled back the rough horse blanket that had been draped over Vernon's body. She let it lay across his neck and shoulders, the skin there now grey and sunken, showing the lines and wrinkles of an aging body. Vernon's mouth hung open; Melody half expected to hear him snore. She would not hear that sound again. Once more her tears fell, as Melody lovingly smoothed Vernon's hair and kissed his forehead.

Abbot had slipped outside, not wanting to intrude on Melody's grief. As the doctor drove away, Roman turned back to Abbot, all of their earlier argument completely forgotten.

"Mitchell could find no evidence of foul play, thankfully."

"Of course not. I shall telephone Franklin's and arrange for them to collect the body as soon as possible. I suggested that the girl stay here until the funeral is over. She is reluctant to sleep in the house but agreed to take the old shepherd's hut instead."

"What, the one in Ribble Top field? Is it still habitable? Good Lord, why would a girl prefer that to a soft bed and indoor plumbing?"

"She is from Emmett. You know how those people live."

"Emmett, eh? That explains a few things."

Abbot raised an eyebrow at his brother.

"Her manner of outfit, her way of speech. Though why they were under Fenny Bridge is a mystery – unless you know?"

"She says they were on their way to Audling. I have the feeling she has not told me the full story, but it hardly seems to matter now."

"I suppose not. If there had been misdeeds afoot, we would have heard about it from the hands. Which reminds me, do you know if any of them are skilled in hedge laying? Ribble Top needs it badly, as does Farley and all along the lane down to Robey. I'd rather not pay more to someone outside if we can set the men to it, but a badly laid hedge is worse than one not laid at all."

"I can lay your hedges." Melody had emerged from the stable and stood behind the brothers as they talked.

Roman and Abbot spun round in unison. Roman spoke first.

"You? It's not a job for a girl. If you need work, we can find you something in the house for a few days."

"I can lay hedges. Granfer taught me, and hurdles. Its not the best time of year for laying though. I can make charcoal too, but I didn't see any kilns in the wood earlier."

"You have the tools?" Abbot was curious.

Melody looked down for a moment, then met his eyes. "I have Granfer's now."

Abbot looked at his brother. "Why not? In exchange for meals and the use of the hut? We'll soon see if she is able."

Roman looked keenly at Melody. She had a substance about her, no frailty or delicate air, and not unattractive. Could a woman manage such a physically demanding job? He knew women had taken over all kinds of industry during the war; he was reluctant to believe that she would do a good job, but since his initial concerns of foul play had been allayed by Doctor Mitchell's examination, he was becoming interested in keeping the young woman around.

"They do need seeing to soon, before the sap rises. We'll give you a week's trial, time enough to see to the funeral. Work hard and well, and we'll keep you on if you wish to stay. Otherwise, after a week, is it Audling you were heading for?"

Melody nodded.

"Then after a week, you can continue on your way."

"That sounds a fair exchange, wouldn't you say?" Abbot asked, unable to keep the hope from his voice.

"It does." Melody held out her hand to Roman to shake on the agreement.

Roman chuckled as he gripped her hand in his own. "You won't be able to do much damage in a week, at least."

"I'll stay with Granfer until the 'taker comes." Melody glanced at Abbot, then turned and re-entered the stables.

"She's a strange one," Abbot said quietly.

"Emmett people are all strange. You'd better telephone Franklin's and see if they can send someone out this afternoon."

Vernon Trow's body was collected by the men from Franklin's undertakers late that afternoon and conveyed to their premises in Robey. Melody had spoken at length with the men about their practices of laying out. It had taken a great deal of reassurance on their part to stop Melody following the motor van to carry out what she felt was necessary herself. With more tears, Melody had watched the motor van slowly leave the yard as dusk fell.

She had eaten a small bowl of leek and potato soup at Cook's kitchen table, and been told to return at seven for her supper. Agnes had been charged with helping Melody carry brooms, bedding and a lamp down to the shepherd's hut, to clean and prepare it as Melody's quarters. Agnes, unlike Cook and Doctor Mitchell, had no prejudiced opinions of those from Emmett. She chattered away in her slow speech while they walked along the lane about how long she had been in service at the farm, about the Cranshaws and other people in Robey whom Melody might meet.

"You're very brave, wanting to sleep out here by yourself. I don't think I would want to." Agnes smoothed the top blanket on the bed platform, then stood up and stretched. "I mean, what happens when you need the lavvy?"

"We had a stool over a pit. I'll make one."

"In the woods? Not even in an outhouse?" Agnes was incredulous at such medieval conditions.

Melody was aware that modern houses had indoor water closets. The Summerton farmhouse had a small bathroom and a separate toilet similar to the Cranshaw's, which Melody had used once or twice, and the new village hall in Emmett Green also had an indoor toilet. Yet in the wood, piped water was a luxury and most families dug latrines a little way from their cabins.

"It's how we live. Lived. There's no drains."

"And what will you do for water?"

"There's a pump in the yard, I'll fill a bucket or two as I need it. With this little stove, all will be well." Melody sat on the bed. Her pack stood next to Vernon's under the small window at the end of the hut. The feeling of numbness had not left her since Franklin's men had taken Vernon away. She did not want to talk, she wanted to sleep.

Agnes was not as perceptive as Abbot had been. She sat next to Melody and looked around the hut.

"I've never been to Audling. I went to Derring once, for their fair day. We all went from school. We had a grand time of it. Have you been to Derring?"

"No. Not to Audling either. Granfer wanted us to go there."

"Why?"

Melody was too tired to be evasive now, and Agnes had been very kind to her. "He said my mother lives there and we should find work there."

Agnes considered this information for a moment.

"My mother is in the asylum."

Melody turned to look at Agnes; she had not expected to hear those words.

Agnes continued, "They put her there when she had my little brother. They said she was immoral, I think that was the word, having children out of wedlock. I don't know who my father is, mother never told me. They put me and my brother Frank in the orphanage for a while, then he was adopted. I don't know where he is now. I was older and no one wanted to adopt me, so they sent me to work here when I was fourteen."

"I'm sorry. I don't know my father either. Granfer and Grammer brought me up. I haven't seen my mother since I was seven."

The two young women sat in silence for a few moments, each considering the other's situation. The lamp flickered in a draught.

Agnes turned to Melody. "So, we're both on our own then."

"We are. But you have a job and a bed. Are you happy here?"

"They are good people to work for. Cook is a little fierce, but we rub along all right."

"And the brothers?"

"Mister Roman has a temper. Not that he has ever raised a hand to me or anything like that. Mister Abbot is quiet. I like him well enough. I spend most of my time seeing to Missus Cranshaw these days."

"And the other men around the farm, are they ..." Melody struggled to think of the word she needed.

"The hands? Mostly from Robey. They are well enough. Some like a drink but they hardly have the money these days. Oh, you mean, do they take advantage?"

Melody agreed, that was what she had meant.

"No. I've known them for years, no one has been anything but polite with me. And you could tell Mister Roman or Mister Abbot if anything like that happened. They'd see whoever it was off the farm just like that." She clicked her fingers.

Melody did not explain that she knew only too well how that might happen.

Once Agnes had gone, and Melody had collected her supper and brought a pail of water down from the yard, she made herself a small mug of weak tea and sat on the top step in the hut doorway looking up at the night sky. There were no stars, which meant the cloud cover would keep the frost at bay. In the near distance, she could hear the sheep moving around the field and an occasional bleat. She was used to being alone in the woods, but never quite this alone. Melody shivered and pulled the blanket more tightly around herself.

MELODY MAKES AN IMPRESSION

VERNON TROW WAS BURIED in Robey churchyard the following Friday. Melody was surprised that both Roman and Abbot Cranshaw accompanied her, respectfully removing their caps and singing the two hymns in faltering quiet voices from the rear of the church. Agnes was permitted to attend the funeral at Melody's request. Melody was still wary of Cook, but had decided that she and Agnes had a common bond and appreciated the young woman's company.

It was Agnes who asked on their return from the church whether there was anyone in Emmett who should be told of Vernon's passing. Melody had not given the subject much thought during that week.

"No. Perhaps in time they will all learn of it, but not now. It's too soon."

Agnes had quickly learned that if Melody did not want to discuss a subject, she could not prise any further comment from her. She wanted to ask why it was too soon, but kept her question to herself.

Melody had made a good start on the hedge. She had walked its length, noting the dominance of blackthorn with dismay. It's vicious needles would require the leather gloves from Vernon's pack and still careful handling. The land rose with the lane towards the farmhouse, which meant Melody began to lay from the highest part away from the edge of the woodland. She foraged in the trees for straight hazel branches to use as staves driven into the ground in between the existing shrubby trees and bushes, and stripped the bark from shorter branches to tie the laid hedge in place. It was important to prepare these in advance so that she would not waste time trudging back and forth through the woodland while working, allowing the bent branches to spring back upwards.

It was still a little early for birds to have begun nesting, but Melody took care to look for any attempts that had been made. A robin sang to her from a short way along the hedge, but for now no other birds came near her.

Another product of her foraging was a stack of much smaller sticks to feed into the little black stove. Melody began each day with a cup of weak tea after visiting the latrine she had dug just inside the woodland edge. Vernon's pocket watch stood on a wooden three-legged stool which Abbot had agreed she could take from the stables. Melody naturally woke around six each morning, long before the eastern skyline began to grow light. She ate a cold breakfast from provisions she brought back the evening before from the kitchen.

Once it was light enough to see without her lamp, Melody carried her tools (Vernon's billhook, a selection of knives and a small saw) along with Vernon's leather gloves along the lane to her place of work for the day. By the end of the first week, she had laid almost fifty feet of hedge. Her arms and face were scratched, her boots had begun to let in water, but the physical activity had helped ease her from the crushing grief she had felt into a tolerable metronomic existence.

Melody had been left largely to herself for that week. Agnes stopped to chat on her half day holiday before continuing into Robey to visit her friends. Abbot came to inspect her progress on the second day, but appeared to Melody to feel awkward as she continued working. As far as she was concerned, she was perfectly able to talk and work at the same time. It was not the way of the people of Emmett, but she did not stop.

Roman Cranshaw also came past later in the week, the day after Vernon's funeral. He rode a glistening black mare who eyed Melody suspiciously and fidgeted from side to side in the lane. It was raining steadily. Roman was splattered with mud from his ride, his face flushed.

"I didn't expect to see you out working in this." He spoke loudly, with a hint of annoyance.

"It's only water," Melody said over her shoulder. "This won't lay itself."

Roman was increasingly perturbed that Melody did not show him the deference he thought he deserved. She had thanked him for arranging the funeral, but only, he felt, as a passing comment when they left the churchyard.

"Will you stop that for a moment."

Melody slowly stood up straight, allowing the branch she had been trimming the underside shoots from to flop over to one side. She wore a leather hat with a wide brim and a leather apron under her jacket. The hat was starting to allow the rain to seep through and a trickle ran down the side of Melody's face. She wiped it away with the back of her hand.

"I can see that you are doing a fair job here. You may as well stay and finish it, unless you plan to leave for wherever you and your grandfather were heading to?"

Melody had not thought too far into the future, but she had on one level enjoyed the feeling of wood in her hands again and felt proud of what she had achieved. It certainly helped her to fall asleep as soon as she laid down each evening.

"I want to finish this. If I leave now, if you don't have someone take over straight away, none of this will make much difference and your sheep will still get through yonder." Melody waved her hand further down the lane.

Roman studied the young woman in front of him. He knew the days when servants knew their place were coming to an end. Men from all walks of life had been thrown together in the trenches and while the rich had bought their sons commissions which elevated them often far above their abilities, the divisions between the lower classes had dissolved in the mud and chaos. There was something about this girl, a self-assurance, which he recognised but was surprised to see in a woman of her age. It was almost as if she did not care whether he threw her off the farm or not, she was only interested in the strip of land in front of them.

"Very well, stay and continue. But for heavens' sake, come to the house when you finish today and have a hot meal and a bath. I don't need another death from exposure to deal with." He turned the horse and trotted off towards the farmhouse.

It was an unnecessary remark. Melody watched the horse for a moment, fighting a wave of sorrow that had swept up out of nowhere. Vernon had taught her to work; he had said that as long as she did a good job, she would always be able to look after herself and could name her price. If she could not return to Emmett, she would stay here while there was work for her to do. That was her price.

Agnes took Melody's soaked clothes that evening to rinse and run through the mangle in the laundry room. Melody had brought a second outfit with her. She had only one other set of clothes; she had never needed a large wardrobe.

Cook was piping icing around the top of a cake. She called out to Agnes from the kitchen.

"Best put those things on the airer. They won't dry out in that old caravan."

"She has a stove in there."

"Hardly enough to keep the frost off. Use the airer. She can come and get them tomorrow; I assume she's staying on for a while?"

"Mister Roman said she could stay and finish working on the hedges."

"No job for a lady." Cook sniffed and piped the final swirl, "But then, there's no ladies in Emmett."

Melody's hair was once again clean. She had brought with her to the house a slender wooden pin which she now pushed through a hole on one side of a scrap of leather, through the twist of hair she held at the back of her head, and then out through a second hole on the opposite end of the leather. It was a versatile accessory, used by the women of Emmett who had not followed the fashion of their cosmopolitan sisters for much shorter hair styles. Roman Cranshaw was at that moment walking along the landing to the stairs to go down for his dinner. He passed the open door of the bathroom and was stopped in his tracks by a glance at Melody's silhouette. Her arms held aloft; her profile as well-proportioned as any woman of class.

Melody froze, seeing Roman out of the corner of her eye. He did not linger but continued on his way downstairs. Melody frowned at her smeared reflection in the mirror. The ways of those who were not woodlanders confused her. She had to be cautious around them.

Abbot was away for a few days visiting an old army friend. The weather had lifted, from grey cold days that hardly got light to bright frosty starts which filled out into increasingly warmer days. Narcissus pushed their way up along the roadsides, their nodding heads resembling gossiping women of old. Abbot had taken the car, as his friend lived beyond the eastern ridge of Wynn Vale and too far for a horse to manage in a single day. This left Roman confined to the farm unless he chose to saddle the black mare and ride out.

He stood at his bedroom window on one of those bright sunny mornings having dressed and shaved before breakfast, and looked out across his land. From such an elevated position, he could see the shepherd's hut in the distance, a wisp of smoke lazily emerging from the little black chimney pipe. Roman admitted to himself that Melody had worked hard on the hedge-laying and had made a good show of it. He had watched her progress, usually from across the pasture or higher up the lane, and had admired her efficiency of movement as he would a horse at a sale.

He watched her now as she descended the steps holding her mug of tea. She sat on the tread; Roman could not see what she was eating, but realised that she was breaking off morsels and throwing them on the ground nearby. After a few moments, a glossy black rook flapped down in front of her. It hunched as it patrolled the grass, periodically stopping to eat one of the small pieces of food Melody had shared.

Roman's first thought was how wasteful Melody was being. If she did not want the food he provided (through Cook's industry), then he must see that her rations were reduced. Melody held out her hand towards the rook. Roman couldn't make out if she held any food, but assumed that she did. The rook cautiously stepped closer, leaning its head to one side then the other. Then with a stretch of its long wings it took flight. It wheeled up and around, then headed off to join its parliament in the tree tops. There was a general flurry of movement as the bird was absorbed into the trees; Roman could hear their raucous cries.

Melody remained on the steps drinking her tea. She was looking out directly towards the house. Roman was confident that she could not see him behind the reflection of clouds and sky on his window. A thought occurred to him: was Melody at that moment thinking of him, as he stood there observing her?

The tea did not stay hot for very long in Melody's enamel mug, especially as she sat in the cold morning air. The animals and birds which inhabited the woodland and the surrounding fields had gradually pierced her muffling shell of grief and Melody now thought of them as cousins of the few she had regularly seen near to the cabin in Emmett. It was a tenuous link to the home she no longer had. In the first couple of days after Vernon's death, Melody had tried her hardest not to think of anything at all. However, as the days unwound towards March, she had allowed herself some tentative mental forays into considering her current and future situation.

Her immediate needs were being adequately met. She had shelter, food, the use of a bathroom if she wanted it, and occupation to tire her physically each day. What she missed was the easy companionship of working side by side with another or a small group. She did not miss chatter, for the woodlanders of

Emmett were not given to talking while they worked. They saved that for evenings or celebration days when they would come together around a fire. Melody missed the sense of community.

She also, she realised, missed Abbot. Though they had not seen each other every day, and not even spoken each time they did see each other, Melody wondered where he was and why he hadn't walked or ridden past down the lane recently. If he had been ill, she was sure Agnes would have mentioned it. Agnes would have been relied upon to minister to the sickbed as the only servant living in besides Cook.

Why did she miss him? He had shown her kindness, without seeming to want anything in return. It was unusual, in Melody's experience.

The precarious mound of government forms and letters on Roman's desk was growing daily. Farming was becoming a bureaucratic nightmare, and it tried his patience sorely despite the income it afforded the Cranshaw family. After Agnes had brought in his morning coffee, Roman found himself thinking once more of Melody. He would be riding to hounds in a few days; he should ask some of the hunt if they knew anything about the girl and her grandfather. Roman was sure she had a good stock line in her heritage somewhere, he refused to believe she was purely Emmett through and through. He smiled to himself. How absurd to be even curious about her in that way! And yet something about her had wormed its way into his blood and he found himself contemplating her more often each day.

His father would not have objected to a marriage outside of their class, Roman was sure. Robert Cranshaw had himself been fortunate to marry above his station; Catherine's father had owned a part share in several Cornish mines, and she had grown up in a large townhouse in Exeter. Roman stopped his train of thought abruptly, his coffee cup less than an inch from his lips. Why was he thinking of marriage?

Abbot was, at that moment, contemplating Melody in connection with his own future. Though many miles from the farm, and thoroughly enjoying his time with his old comrade James, Melody had frequently appeared in his mind's eye during his visit. James' sister, Isobel, had also frequently appeared, though very much in the flesh. Like thousands of her age across the country, the lack of eligible (and whole) young men had prompted more forward behaviour than their mothers had ever had to countenance.

Isobel was there at every meal; she was there on the tennis court, at the theatre, giving the recital, strolling along the river and riding bicycles across the heath. She tried demure, then loud, coquettish then brazen. Abbot knew exactly what was going on and had it happened just six weeks before he might have been ensnared. But that was before he had found Melody.

The day before Abbot was due to return to Wynn Vale, on a rare occasion when he found himself alone with James, Abbot voiced his confusion to his friend.

"... So you see, I know next to nothing about her, and she is not the most beautiful or wealthy or even vivacious young woman I know, yet she has become embedded in my mind and I can think of no other. It is hopeless!"

"I won't lie, it has been rather amusing to watch Isobel try so hard to gain your attention this week. Now I understand your evasiveness, I am sure she will not languish for too long once you've returned home. But look here old chap, is this Melody girl really someone who would fit into your life? You say you know nothing of her; I hope you don't see yourself as some kind of Professor Higgins figure!"

They were on the local golf course, which still refused women entry. Abbot shouldered his bag of clubs and waited for James to take his put before they continued to the next tee.

"Honestly, I don't know. I don't even know how to talk to her, to speak her language as it were." They walked along the fairway, nodding to other players as they passed.

"I think before you make an absolute ass of yourself, you should at least try to find out why they left their home. There could be an innocent explanation of course, but it does sound a rather odd situation. Look here, she's not pregnant, is she?" James looked up at Abbot as he placed his golf ball on the tee. They had been through much together, and James hoped Abbot had not already made a fool of himself in that respect.

"Not that I know of, no. I suppose it could be possible. Good Lord, do you think that could be why they were on the road?"

"Can you even be sure the man she was with was her true grandfather?" James addressed the ball and shouted, "Four!"

"Oh, good shot! Well, she called him 'Granfer' which is a common term in the Vale. But I'd feel a cad to ask her outright if he really was."

James picked up the tee and spoke to it rather than looking directly at Abbot.

"Caddish or not, you're going to have to ask her what's been going on."

Abbot knew his friend was right. But how to engage Melody in that kind of conversation when they had only exchanged the briefest of words so far? What if it caused her to run away? Abbot did not want that to happen. He would need to take a slow and cautious approach to it all. Roman had agreed to keep her on the farm; there was no hurry to get a little closer to this mysterious young woman, Abbot decided.

Gathering Information

Holden Prentice stood in the lane, with forty-five fox hounds excitedly milling about, yipping and salivating while the horses were being mounted in the courtyard. As second gamekeeper, Holden Prentice was not invited to ride with the hunt. His father, as bailiff, had declined his invitation. Edmund Prentice was not fond of horses and could not reconcile his distrust of them with his desire to improve his position in the local society. His wife had tried to encourage him to put aside his nervousness, but without success. She had to be satisfied that her son held an important duty when the hunt convened at Marchett House; he was responsible for bringing the hounds into the lane and counting them all back into the kennels at the end of their exertions.

The horses with their riders in red and black jackets began to move out into the lane. Holden nodded to those he knew, keeping one eye on the hounds as they started to sniff in earnest along the hedgerow. Snatches of conversation came to him through the noise of the dogs and hooves.

"... yes, do let me know when you will be going up to town again, I shall get you tickets..."

"... well of course, he never did tell his wife where he'd been, the old dog!"

"... Melody? Such an unusual name. Yes, I believe there was a young girl called that who lived in the woods until only a few weeks ago. If it's the girl I'm thinking of, rumour has it she behaved with impropriety with one of the young men on the Estate. Told to vacate their property immediately. Good thing too! Can't have that kind of behaviour when so many children are present..."

Holden Prentice focused on the two men who were conversing to his left. Phillip Turner had lived in Emmett Green for many years, running the school and the village Boy Scout pack. As the man he was talking to turned his horse, Holden recognised him as Roman Cranshaw. Why would Cranshaw be asking about Melody Trow? Holden had heard that the Trows had been heading for Audling and had assumed they had arrived to be absorbed into the bloated industrial grime of the city. The Cranshaw's farm was only twenty miles of so from the northern end of Emmett wood. Holden decided to ask some of his own contacts to see if anyone had heard of an old man and young girl seeking work beyond the woodland.

Abbot had no interest in hunting. While he accepted the damage that foxes could do to a chicken run or to young lambs, he still did not wish to chase across the landscape in pursuit of one.

He did not approve of the way the hounds were encouraged to rip apart their quarry, or worse still, if the hounds lost the scent when the fox had been injured, the wild animal would suffer an unnecessarily long, slow death from infection or starvation. Abbot liked to ride, but not to hunt.

He decided to take advantage of the good weather to make his first approach to Melody since his return to the farm. On the pretext of wanting to know how much longer it would be before the sheep could be moved back to the Ribble Top field where Melody's hut was stationed, he whistled to himself as he strolled down the lane from the stable yard. Melody was already at work. She had reached a patch of brambles which she needed to clear before she could continue to lay the hedge. They were proving vicious, snagging her clothes and piercing her leather gloves and apron every time she tried to cut them away from her path.

Abbot stopped a little way up the lane and watched Melody for a few moments. She had begun to wear a pair of Vernon's trousers when the rain and mud had exhausted her own supply of clothes, and continued to as she found them far more practical. With her hair caught up in a twist with the leather band and wooden pin, her hat shading her neck and eyes, one could have been forgiven for thinking she was just another farm hand. Suddenly she stood up, clutching a long length of bramble, and looked straight at Abbot as if she had known all along he was watching her. He could not suppress a smile as he continued walking towards her.

"Those look nasty."

"I'll burn them in the stove. They'll soon grow back again, but I need them gone for now." Melody was trying to ignore the little flutter in her stomach as Abbot came to within a few feet of her.

"It's coming along nicely. How long until you've finished this stretch do you think?"

"Two or three days. Cutting this all out doesn't help. You want to bring the ewes back in."

"Yes, the ones not in lamb." Abbot tried not to stare at Melody. His mouth was suddenly dry and everything else he had thought to say to her had evaporated from his mind.

Melody waited for a moment. She wasn't sure if Abbot was looking critically at her work, or if his mind were elsewhere and he had forgotten she was there.

"I was going to stop for a drink. It's hot. Would you like some water?"

Abbot swallowed and hoped his voice would not betray him. "Yes, that would be a good idea. You're right, it's much warmer this morning than I had anticipated."

Melody led the way through the gate and up to the hut. She pushed the brambles under the hut next to her pile of kindling, then climbed the steps and took up her enamel mug. She dipped it into the pail of water then turned and offered it to Abbot.

He took a sip. "Are you not having some too?"

"I only have one mug."

Abbot's embarrassment coloured his cheeks. He drank half the water then handed the mug back to Melody who finished it without wiping the rim. While she returned the mug to the narrow shelf above the bed, Abbot gave himself a shake. There was no reason to be so tongue-tied in front of such a young girl! James had suggested he start with a simple question of her future plans. If Melody was keen to move on, Abbot would not make an idiot of himself only to have it broadcast across the county.

"Look here, once all this is finished, do you think you will want to stay here?"

Melody still hadn't quite got the measure of the dynamic between the brothers, and which of them had the ultimate say over farm matters. She thought it must be Roman as the eldest, but she had seen both brothers give instruction to the hands and Agnes had said on several occasions that Abbot had made decisions on this and that. She was thinking of her answer when Abbot continued.

"I wondered if you might return to your home, to Emmett, or perhaps go further afield?"

At the mention of Emmett, Melody looked to the ground. "I shan't be going back to Emmett."

"Oh? You don't have family or friends there still? I know there was no one at the funeral, but that was so hastily arranged..."

"I have friends but no family. If there is no work for me here, I will go on yonder."

It occurred to Abbot that Melody did not add a deferential 'sir' when addressing him, as the farm hands and the house staff always did.

"It is unusual for a woman to be skilled in field crafts. Are all the women of Emmett so well accounted for?"

Melody sighed. She had been able to avoid Agnes' probing questions, but it seemed that Abbot was determined to learn more about her and her people. She could detect no hint of scorn in his voice, or annoyance as she had in Roman's. Abbot spoke kindly to all the hands, as if they were old friends. Would Abbot still want to be her friend once he knew the ways of the woodlanders?

"You want to know how we live?"

"Yes, if you are willing to tell me. It's strange, being only fifteen or so miles away, yet I have never had reason to travel there or met anyone who was brought up there. We always have business in Audling and naturally look northwards.”

“People tell stories about us.”

“Indeed they do. I would rather hear the truth.”

“I should get back to work.” She made no attempt to move. It was more of a question than a statement, the inflection in her voice asking Abbot’s permission to stay.

“A few minutes won’t hurt, surely. I won’t tell my brother if you don’t.” He smiled, hoping to reassure her.

Melody went into the hut and came out with the stool. “The ground is damp still.”

Abbot thanked her and lowered himself onto the stool a little way from the steps, where Melody sat and stretched her legs out in front of her.

She told him of growing up in Emmett wood with Vernon and Avens. She explained how the families grew and shrank with each passing year, how homes were passed on just like tools and other possessions. The homes were theirs, but the land was not. Melody told of the Candlemas awakening with the Mummers and the long summer nights with fireflies lighting the paths between the clearings. She explained that the youngest children went to the school in Emmett Green, but once they were ten or eleven years old most had stopped attending and were helping their families in whatever industry they were known for. Some went to the sawmills or the papermill, some out to the farms, and some of the girls had traditionally gone into service but those days were now at an end and most stayed in the cabins until a man (young or otherwise) caught their eye.

Melody mentioned Cicely briefly, along with the few people of her own age that she would spend time with when their work was over for the day. She talked of the stories that Cicely’s Grammer told, from when the old Queen was a young bride. As the sun climbed in the sky, she told Abbot of how Vernon had taken her to help him lay hedges and over time had taught her all he knew.

Abbot listened as if he were back in school with the teacher regaling the boys of some historical battle. Yet he knew there were no embroidered details in Melody's tale. Her voice lifted and fell with emotion, she blinked back tears as she remembered her grandmother. When she came to a natural pause, she stood up and took another mugful of water from the pail. It had been a long time since she had talked this much to anyone. She drank half from the mug then offered it to Abbot.

When it was empty and she had gone back into the cabin, Abbot decided to ask one of the two questions that had been playing most on his mind since his conversations with James.

"If your grandparents raised you, what happened to your parents?"

Melody looked at Abbot from the doorway of the cabin. She felt she could trust him, at least as much as she did Agnes.

"My mother left me with Granfer and Grammer. She hadn't always been with us in the cabin. Granfer said she lives in Audling, but I don't know. Grammer died when I was seven. I've not seen my mother since then."

"And your father?"

"I don't know that either."

Abbot took a deep breath, then let it out slowly. There was nothing Melody had said so far that gave him reason to think she was lying, or to raise his suspicions about her. Being the product of an unmarried liaison was unfortunate; Abbot was not one to blame the child in these situations. Melody had told him consistently that she and Vernon had been heading to Audling, and now the location of her mother added some substance to that. Abbot decided to plough on with his questions.

"I can understand now why you were reluctant to stay in the house, how you might be more comfortable in familiar surroundings here." He nodded at the hut, "But what I don't understand is why you and your grandfather would leave what sounds like a perfectly serviceable cabin and walk for two or three days to Audling with no accommodation along the way, in the middle of winter."

"We had to leave."

Abbot waited. Melody sat back down on the steps and put her head in her hands for a moment, then looked up and pushed the lose strands of hair away from her face.

"The Bailiff said we had to leave. I ... I had a fight with his son."

Abbot's eyebrows showed his surprise.

"A fight? What about?"

Melody bit her lip. This was it. This was where she could either lie and hope she wouldn't be found out or tell the truth and be told to leave again. She would have to go to Audling, to look for her mother and hope she would take Melody in.

"He sat with us after the Mummers had finished, with Cicely and me and our friends, and when I said I wanted to go home, he said he would walk back with me. It was on his way. I thought he was just being a friend, he's sometimes sat and talked with us before, but really he doesn't like us woodlanders. But I said all right, and when we got back to the cabin he wanted to kiss me. I didn't want him to. We had a fight. Granfer came out, and he told Holden to go. Then the next day Holden came back with his father and they gave Granfer a paper that said we had to leave by the end of the day after."

The words tumbled out. Abbot could see Melody had begun to shake, her breathing coming in gulps. He was more concerned about her physical reaction than about the substance of what she had just told him in that moment. He stood up, wanting to comfort Melody. At the same time, Melody stood up and went backwards up one step towards the hut door, her hand raised as if to stop Abbot approaching. He stopped and raised his own hands to indicate he would go no further. Slowly he sat back down, his elbows on his knees and concern clearly showing on his face.

"It sounds rather unfair, to put someone out of their home on the basis of an altercation."

"The Estate owns the wood."

"Yes, I see that. I can also see that being bested by a woman would hurt a chap's pride, possibly more than any physical blow you may have landed." Abbot felt it had been a particularly vindictive action on the part of the Estate Agent. He wondered if there were a history of bad feeling between the families and that this was somehow a boiling point. He decided that it did not matter. In his opinion, a woman was entitled to withhold intimacy if she wished to.

Melody watched Abbot closely, waiting for him to tell her to pack her things.

"I'd better be getting along. Mother gets agitated if she is left alone for too long." He got up again to leave, then paused, "I wonder ... it's a beautiful day today, but the forecast is for rain. Perhaps when it does, you could come up to the house and sit with Mother for a while? I will introduce you, of course. She says very little these days, in truth I'm not sure that she takes in a lot of what goes on around her, but to have someone to sit with her, perhaps read to her ... you can read?"

Melody nodded.

"Well, come up to the house when the weather turns. We'll see how things work out." Abbot smiled and began to make his way back along the field edge to the gate.

Melody watched him retreating, bewildered. How had that exchange not resulted in her being told to leave? She had heard Agnes talk about Mrs Cranshaw, and of how she spent most of her time sitting in the drawing room gazing out of the window across the fields. Agnes thought Mrs Cranshaw was still waiting for her oldest son David to return from France, but that would never happen. Melody considered Abbot's offer, for her to sit with his mother when the weather was not conducive to working outside. She had never minded the rain or the variances of winter, but perhaps it would be nice to be inside a big house while the windows were battered with hailstones.

Roman Cranshaw held his glass of Madeira aloft for the toast. It had been an exhilarating ride across the southern downs of Wynn Vale that morning, and he had been able to establish some of the reason why Vernon and Melody Trow had left Emmett. Piecing together a comment here and a supposition there, he had come to the conclusion that the Trows had been hard done by.

Melody's behaviour had been described as anywhere between a playful shove to a full-blown sordid encounter. Roman had regarded Holden Prentice from across the yard as they returned, and appraised the young man as sullen and rather arrogant. The looks that Holden gave the riders, Roman included, had not been disguised; there was a definite air of conceit about the man. To be spurned in his affections would naturally draw his wrath. Yet Roman also understood the attraction of Melody, if indeed Holden had felt it. She was a handsome woman, not slender and delicate as many of the landed women folk were.

Yes, she would bear strong children one day, he thought, then shook his head at the way his own thoughts had led him.

GETTING CLOSER

THE WEATHER HELD FOR another week. Melody had finished the main stretch of hedge that separated the lane from Ribble Top field, and had begun to lay the portion perpendicular to the lane which followed the rise and fall of the meadow southwards. The days were slowly lengthening and soon the Equinox moon would rise up from the sea and glow like a penny in the night sky above the southern Vale.

Melody woke earlier and earlier with the rising birdsong. The rook still did not trust her enough to eat from Melody's hand, but it now tapped on the door of the shepherd's hut if she were slow to open it. Then it flapped lazily just a few feet away and regarded Melody with its blue-black eyes, hunched like a monk and waiting for the morsels she threw onto the grass. Melody had named the bird Archer, after the sound of its call.

One evening at dusk, when Melody had bathed and eaten her supper at the farmhouse, Roman Cranshaw was in the garden smoking as Melody emerged from the kitchen door. She carried a bundle of clothes which Agnes had washed and dried for her, and some bread and two cold boiled eggs for her breakfast.

"Good evening. The sky is red, but I think there is only one more dry day to be had before the rain arrives. What do you think?" Roman exhaled like a smouldering dragon.

"I'm surprised that it's been dry for so long, being March."

Again, Roman thought, no pleasantries, no deference, and yet no arrogance or rudeness in the girl.

"Here, let me carry that for you. I could do with a stroll. I spend far too much time at my desk these days." He held out his hand to take Melody's bundle.

She frowned but handed it over. The path down to the lane through the rose garden was wide enough to walk two abreast. Roman had been deliberately waiting for Melody, having seen her walk up the lane to the house an hour before. It had given him time to prepare his opening move.

"Are you interested in flowers, or vegetables, or are you only concerned with trees?"

"I like flowers, though we don't ... we never grew them like this." Melody gestured to the rose bushes, some of which had buds forming at the end of dark red shoots.

"Tell me what flowers grow in the woodland."

Melody looked at Roman to see if he were making fun of her. He kept looking straight ahead.

"Well... some only grow for a short while, and some plants flower before the fruits or berries come, so the flowers are just to attract the bees. Bluebells and cowslips come in the spring, you've some bluebells in the wood, I think. Celandines too, those are the yellow flowers. Then anemone, violets and stitchwort, foxgloves, herb Robert. Honeysuckle smells nice, that grows on the edge of the wood. It doesn't like it too dark."

Roman nodded, as a kindly teacher would when a pupil recited the alphabet. "And tell me of the trees," he prompted.

"Your wood here is much like Emmett. You have beech, hazel, ash and birch. Oaks need more space, but you have some in the fields yonder. There's some rowan along the lane and most of your hedge is blackthorn." Melody suddenly became self-conscious of the scratches up her arms. The leather gloves only protected her hands.

"What would you do with the woodland, if it belonged to you?"

"I don't understand..."

"If you owned the wood here, does it need thinning? Are there trees that could be felled for timber? Should it be cleared and turned over to pasture or crops of some kind? You have spent some time there, how should it be managed?"

This was the test Roman had decided upon. He had admitted to himself that he found Melody attractive, both in her physical appearance but also her practical abilities and lack of fawning and simpering. He assumed she had a rudimentary formal education but he wanted to establish what level of intelligence Melody possessed. He knew from his time in the army that formal education often meant little when a practical response was required.

They had now reached the gateway to the lane. Roman stepped back to allow Melody to pass through first. This necessitated a physical proximity which was brief, but allowed him to smell the scent of the soap she had recently used. Melody was thinking of a reply and did not acknowledge Roman as she moved past him. As they turned into the lane, the sun was melting into the downs to the west. The bell of Robey church proclaimed evensong to the handful of parishioners who regularly placed their coins in the collection dish.

"There are some older trees that would make good timber. The ash are good and straight, some beech too. You could coppice the hazel, someone has done in the past. Depends what you want to do with the branches. I haven't seen any charcoal kilns."

"I think there used to be some nearer to Robey but they tell me Emmett charcoal is the best in any case. Could we sell the hazel to the people there?"

"If you weren't to use it for hurdles or baskets."

"And if we did coppice the hazel, how long before we could do so again? How quickly does it grow?"

Melody was relaxing into the conversation now. It was a topic she implicitly understood.

"You would only coppice some the first year. If you took it all, you'd have to wait another ten years or so before you could take more from the same tree. In Emmett we work in a circle. Like a clock, every year we take from the trees at the next part of the circle. If we start at twelve o'clock, the next year we'd coppice the one o'clock trees, then the next year the two o'clock trees. That gives them a chance to grow again in between. Do you see?"

Roman smiled, "Yes, I see. I have been considering selling the woodland to the Forestry Commission. They would take on the management – we could concentrate on the pasture and perhaps bring in some beef cattle. The alternative is more paperwork, but to take their Woodland Grant to help pay for the management, and then they clear the timber."

"You would give up the wood?"

"It was much larger before the war. You might not have ventured to the western edge, but it continued for another ten or twelve miles. My father made a significant amount selling it to the Commission. It seems they are keen to buy up more parcels of land; they keep sending me letters practically begging me to sell."

Melody was quiet for a moment. She knew about trees, but she knew little about the workings of government or finance. Vernon had provided for his family and Melody had rarely needed, or even seen, money.

"Do you want to sell it?" She finally asked.

"The trouble with selling land, Melody, is that the buyer can then do as they please with it. We sold the portion in the west because we could not see it from the house. There was access from the Derring road, no increase in traffic between here and Robey. But if we were to sell the rest, well, you can see clearly from here how it might change the view.

"The issue then becomes, would the financial benefit outweigh the inconvenience. I believe we can coppice without the Commission's approval, though if we were to fell the larger trees, they would require reports and what not. Yet at this point in time, we are making no money at all from the wood, so if the hazel could generate a little income, it would become more attractive to keep it."

"Do your farm hands know how to coppice?"

"I expect they could be taught."

"If you're going to do it, you should make a start now. It's already starting to bud."

"And if we did not, when would it be possible again?"

Melody screwed up her nose, "We don't cut when the leaves are still on. Hazel gets sticky in the summer with the bugs on it."

They were almost at the shepherd's hut. Roman would be returning to the house in the dark. Their footsteps slowed to a stop as they reached the field gate and they both turned to watch the last of the orange leave the sky.

"We are lucky to live in such a beautiful county, don't you think?" Roman asked quietly.

"I don't know anywhere else. I don't think I want to live in a town though, or a city."

"You didn't want to go to Audling?"

"No."

"Are you sure you wouldn't be happier staying in the house? With our family? With me?"

Melody turned towards Roman, only to find him closer than she had expected. She knew she was lonely; she knew no one else would care how she chose to live her life now. Roman stepped forward, placed a hand on her shoulder and kissed her, briefly, before stepping back again and handing out the bundle of clothes for Melody to take. It had been quick, and it had ended before Melody could protest. She did not feel that she wanted to protest if it should happen again.

"Goodnight, Melody." Roman left her standing on the edge of the lane with the bats circling and diving above her.

When Agnes passed by the shepherd's hut the next day on her way to Robey, Melody was sitting on the steps, whittling a small spoon with her short knife.

"It's not like you to be sitting down!"

"I needed to do something else with my hands for a while." Melody stood up, brushed the shavings from her lap and reached inside the hut to bring out the little stool for Agnes.

"Mister Roman and Mister Abbot are arguing again. They've been at it all morning. I'm that glad to be out of the house for a bit."

"Seems like they argue a lot."

"They have been lately, more than ever. The slightest thing sets them off. Then one will slam the door and storm off, usually Mister Abbot. It's a wonder Mrs Cranshaw doesn't say something about it, but you know how she is these days."

"Abbot asked me to go and talk to her when the weather turns."

"Did he? I should think she'll like that."

"You wouldn't mind?"

"Oh, it's not really in my duties, but I've plenty to be getting on with if you did come up to the house. Does that mean you'll be staying a bit longer?"

There was a pause, then Melody asked, "Agnes, if you like someone, a man, how do you know if they like you or if they just want ... other things?"

Agnes leaned forwards, elbows on knees, "You got a sweetheart? You're a dark horse! I didn't think there was anyone you spoke to around here! It's not Kenny Foster is it?"

The idea was so absurd to Melody, she laughed loud and long, much to Agnes' surprise. Kenny Foster, day labourer on the farm, was at least six inches shorter than Melody and twice her age, with a slow manner of speech and movement. Melody would never be unkind to him, but he was not a credible contender for her affections. When she had composed herself again, she shook her head at Agnes and smiled.

"It's not Kenny Foster. It's not anyone, I was just wondering." *And I wish I could ask Cicely but you're the only one here I can talk to,* Melody added to herself. There had been no mistaking Holden Prentice's intentions, but with Roman, Melody was much less sure. And then there was Abbot.

"Well," Agnes seemed to swell with pride at being considered a valuable source of information rather than a chatterbox for once. "I should say, if a man likes to talk to you about things, even boring things, he must feel something towards you. He might give you a gift, like some flowers or some chocolates. But not all the time – that would be like he was paying to spend time with you, and we all know what that leads to." The look of propriety on Agnes' face almost started Melody laughing again, but she disguised it with a cough.

"There have been no gifts."

"Does he hang around, making a nuisance of himself? Do you tell him to go away, even when you wouldn't mind if he stayed?"

Melody almost fell into Agnes' trap but caught herself just in time. "There is no one, Agnes, I was just wondering how I would know if it ever happens."

Agnes did not believe her, but knew better than to push for more details.

The latest argument between the Cranshaw brothers had been over Abbot's invitation to Melody to sit with their mother. Roman was furious that Abbot had not discussed it with him first. Abbot replied that Roman rarely sat with their mother so why did he care who did? Old coals were raked over and as Agnes had told Melody, Abbot stormed out with a slam of the study door. He marched to the stables, saddled his old mare, a chocolate brown fifteen-year-old with a black mane and tail, brushing the offers of help from the stable lad aside gruffly, and cantered out of the yard.

Abbot rode up to the main road, then kept in line with it until he reached the stream at Fenny bridge. There he slowed and allowed the mare to catch her breath and drink from the stream. He knew Roman had been right, he should have discussed it before making the offer to Melody. But he had wanted her to stay at the farm, and give her a reason to spend more time in the house. He wanted to spend more time with her, he knew that now if it had ever been in doubt.

The mare plodded along the side of the stream, heading down towards Robey. Abbot allowed her to determine his course. How to woo the girl, that was the question. He chuckled at himself for using such an old-fashioned word, but the issue was a perplexing one. She was unlike any of the girls he had known, both there in Wynn Vale and across the sea in France. He was still mulling it over when the mare reached the first cottage in Robey, and Abbot decided to stop at The Bellows inn for a half pint of bitter and some cold pie if they had any.

Holden Prentice had made excuses and taken the afternoon off work. He had made more excuses, and outright lies, and managed to convince an acquaintance to lend him a horse for the rest of the day. He had not wanted to walk all the way to the Cranshaw's farm and then have to walk back again. One day he would own a motor car, but for now, a borrowed horse was better than shanks' pony.

He rode out on the Derring-Audling road, then turned off before the Cranshaw's farm came into sight. Holden thought it unlikely that anyone would recognise him as he crossed the fields. He had a story ready just in case; he was looking for one of the hounds which had been separated from the pack and could be injured. What he had not decided, was exactly what he would do or say if he came upon Melody. He felt compelled to see her; he had woken several times over the past few weeks with Melody's face looming in his dreams. Each time he had wanted to strike her again, to exert his authority over her and bend her to his will. Yet in his waking hours, that desire had faded to simply wanting to look upon her face and hear her voice.

Holden had criss-crossed the fields for a couple of hours and was about to give up his quest, when he spotted the shepherd's hut in the distance. Instinctively he felt its similarity to the caravans that the woodlanders used meant Melody must be nearby. He urged his borrowed horse onwards to the field gate on the far side of the pasture and tied it to the post. Then he set off on foot, to make a quiet and stealthy approach.

Melody judged by the position of the sun that it must be nearing five o'clock. She had not gone back to working on the hedge after Agnes had continued down the lane to Robey. Instead, she now had three rough wooden spoons. There would be nothing wrong in using them as they were, but Melody wanted to see if there was any sandpaper in the workshop next to the stables. Her plan was to make the spoons as smooth as she could, then present them to Cook as a gesture of thanks for the food and drink she had provided Melody with. Even though it had been under Abbot's instruction, Melody felt Cook had slowly become more accepting of her and less caustic in her remarks about the people of Emmett, at least in Melody's hearing.

She had saved some of the shavings to help start the fire in the little black stove, should it go out. These were now in a small basket Melody had made from some split hazel rods. It was rough work but served its purpose. It never occurred to Melody to take pride in the things she made; baskets, spoons, bowls and stools were made as the need arose, as practical objects. Their aesthetic value was inconsequential to Melody. People would buy or trade for them if they wanted them or needed them. All that mattered was that they were fit for purpose.

Holden was approaching the hut from the south, slowly and carefully, staying close to the laid hedge. He became aware of the sound of hooves in the lane on the other side of the hedge, and stopped, crouching down low so as not to be seen. He watched as a young man came at a walk up from Robey. The man looked unsteady in the saddle. Holden thought he might be drunk.

Abbot would have disputed that description. Yes, he had drunk more than a half pint at The Bellows, but he had eaten ham and egg pie and a bowl of rice pudding with a large spoonful of damson jam in the centre. This, Abbot felt, had more than compensated for the three more half pints of beer he had consumed that afternoon while playing shove ha'penny and Grab with a couple of elderly villagers. Now he was simply weary and hoped to take a bath and forty winks before dinner. The mare knew the way home; all Abbot had to do was stay upright. He smelled wood smoke and realised he was passing the shepherd's hut, just as Melody came through the field gate into the lane.

Holden Prentice had crept a little closer to the hut, staying behind the horse and rider. He could hear someone moving about inside, and had seen the faint curl of smoke from the little black chimney. Now he peered around the back corner of the hut as Melody walked across the grass to the gate. He realised he was holding his breath. It was unmistakeably Melody Trow. The horse and rider had stopped; Holden risked moving closer to hear the exchange of words.

Melody had also heard the horse approaching, and had a moment of torment when she realised she did not know who she hoped to see – Roman or Abbot Cranshaw. Her talk with

Agnes had been of small use to her, only confirming that either of the brothers might have the beginnings of some affection for her. Yet as she stepped into the lane and saw Abbot sitting a little too forwards on the mare, her stomach gave another flutter. She smiled up at him.

"Melody!" He called, "Melody, Melody, Melody... a sight for sore eyes."

"You've been drinking."

"Yes, yes I have. And now I am going home."

"I'll walk up with you."

She stepped forward, and as the mare began to walk again Abbot slid even further forward, his face in the horse's mane. Melody thought he might fall and caught hold of the reins in one hand and his shoulder with the other. Abbot lifted his head and grinned at her; she could smell the beer on his breath.

"You caught me! Damned slippery, this saddle. But I am alright, Melody, Melody. Look I can sit up straight like the good soldier I am ... was..." He tried to sit upright, but with his feet out in front, he began to loll backwards instead. The mare side stepped, not understanding the instructions she was receiving down the reins.

"The sooner you're home the better. Come on now." Melody spoke to the mare and pulled it gently forwards as Abbot steadied himself once more.

It was a ten-minute walk along the lane, and closer to five minutes if the pathway through the garden was taken. Melody steered the mare with confidence, every few paces looking back and up at Abbot to make sure he had not fallen off. For his part, he was playing up his inebriation and enjoying the attention Melody was giving him. His vantage point gave him a good view of her back, with her hair caught in its usual twist on the back of her head. He wondered how it would feel to run his fingers through her hair, the golden threads catching the fading light of the sun behind them.

Holden Prentice was also following some feet behind the pair. He was curious as to who the young man was, and why Melody was so familiar with him. Perhaps the stories about Betony Trow had been true and Melody was taking after her mother. Conscious that he had left his borrowed horse some way behind, Holden stopped following when he reached an elm growing at an angle just inside the hedgerow. Standing on its misshaped bole, he was able to watch the man on the horse as they approached the farmhouse. Holden deduced that it must be one of the Cranshaw brothers; he had heard there were three. So, Melody had ingratiated herself with the landowners, he thought. That was not what he had hoped the outcome of their banishment would be. And where was the old man?

Holden turned and made his way back to the gate where he had tied his mount. He was allowing his annoyance to develop and fester. By the time he was back in the saddle, Holden was angry. That girl needed taking down a few pegs, swanning around as if she was lady of the manor!

Melody led the mare round to the stables and handed the reins to one of the stable boys who was just finishing spreading fresh straw in the stalls. Abbot slid out of the saddle and steadied himself against the horse.

"Come in and say hello to Mother." It didn't sound to Melody like a request. She patted the mare's neck and joined Abbot. He stuck out his elbow, an invitation for her to take his arm. He raised an eyebrow, making such a comical face that Melody couldn't help giggling. She slipped her hand under his arm, and the crossed the yard with Abbot swaying gently and Melody attempting to keep him on track.

"I should go in through the kitchen," she said as they reached the front door.

"Nonsense! We shall go in together." He pushed open the door and indicated that Melody should enter first.

They found Catherine Cranshaw in her usual seat in the drawing room. It would be another half hour before dinner was served.

"Mother! Look who I have brought to see you! It's our new ... well, this is Melody. Say hello, Melody."

"Hello Mrs Cranshaw, nice to meet you."

Catherine Cranshaw looked vacantly at Abbot and then at Melody. Melody frowned at Abbot. Abbot rocked gently from side to side like a child's tower of bricks. One shove and he'll fall over, thought Melody. Then recognition seemed to come to Catherine.

"Rosemary?"

"No, Mother, Melody. Look here, perhaps she could read to you. Something from one of your favourites?" Abbot turned a little too quickly and stumbled his way across the room to a bookshelf. As he looked for a familiar novel, Catherine spoke once again, this time in a much quieter, almost pleading voice.

"Rosemary?"

Melody was familiar with the distress that older people sometimes felt when their senses were leaving them. Several of the elderly inhabitants of Emmett had taken to wandering over the years and the children had been enlisted to bring them home; it often seemed that the elders related more readily to the children and were more willing to take their hands and be led back to safety. Melody pulled a chair closer and sat next to Catherine in the dusk-filled room.

"Hello, Mrs Cranshaw. Shall I read for a while?"

A smile broke out across the older woman's face, transforming her into what Melody felt must have been her beautiful younger self. Abbot handed Melody a copy of a much-thumbed novel with a dark blue hard cover, and muttering about needing to wash for dinner, left them alone.

Intruder

It became a habit for Melody to walk up to the farmhouse a little earlier, and spend half an hour or so with Catherine Cranshaw every couple of days. The older woman still called Melody "Rosemary", but Melody didn't mind. Sometimes she read to Catherine, other times she described what she had seen and done that day. Catherine rarely showed any animated interest; she sat silently, hands in her lap, but looking intently at Melody as she spoke. Then Agnes would come in and take Catherine through to the dining room for the evening meal and Melody would go back to the kitchen for hers.

Roman Cranshaw sometimes lingered in the drawing room doorway when Melody was sitting with his mother. He liked the way Melody's voice rose and fell. He liked knowing she was there in the house. Abbot also liked knowing the Melody was close by. Sometimes Abbot would contrive to be walking along the lane at about the time he thought Melody might be ready to make her way to the house. Then they would walk together. An easy friendship was growing between them which Abbot hoped would be a good foundation for more.

Yet he could not think of an appropriate way to broach the subject with Melody. Though she was more relaxed in his company, he often felt she was as skittish as a young mare and might shy away or kick out if he got too close.

Roman had no such concerns. The more he listened to Melody, the more he watched her progress taming the hedgerow, the more attractive she was becoming as a potential mate. He was not interested in a woman who would want to sit and sew or have tea parties. He wanted a woman with whom he could hold a conversation, about the farm or any other topic of his choosing, without the need to explain every minute detail only to receive an inconsequential response in return. Of course, there was much that Melody did not know, but that could be put right with access to newspapers, books and the endless leaflets that the Commission sent him. He knew she could read and write, and that she could grasp concepts quickly. That Melody was pleasant to look at was all the more reason to keep her on the farm for as long as possible.

To this end, one afternoon as Melody was replacing a book on the bookshelf that she had just finished reading to Catherine Cranshaw and preparing to take her dinner in the kitchen, Roman Cranshaw came into the drawing room. Melody turned and caught her breath in surprise.

"Elvers! I didn't hear you; you gave me a fright!"

"Forgive me. I wanted to catch you before you left this evening. I have something for you."

He held forward a small box. It had taken him several hours of thought to decide on a gift that Melody could make use of and would appreciate. Not for her the usual trinkets of a bracelet or necklace. Once he had thought of the gift, and been able to purchase it, he was keen to present it to her as soon as possible. He was aware that she and Abbot were spending more time together as the days grew longer.

"What is it?"

"Take it. Open the box and see."

Melody was hesitant. Agnes' words came back to her. Was this the gift that would become payment in exchange for an expectation of intimacy? Melody looked up at Roman. His smile seemed genuine, not leering or suggestive. She tentatively took the box from his hand.

Removing the lid, inside Melody saw a silver oblong with rounded corners, approximately four inches by one. The hallmark was stamped to the left, and to the right, the maker's name had been engraved in wildly ornate lettering. It sat on a leather pouch with a drawstring at one end, designed to keep the object safe while not in use. It was a penknife.

Melody glanced up again at Roman, then replaced the lid of the box.

"Thank you, but I can't take this. I'd be afraid to lose it."

"Nonsense. See here." He took the box from her and opened it again, taking out the penknife. "It has two blades of Sheffield steel, and this, look, this opens here and is a nail file. I thought you might find that useful as well as the blades?" He opened each tool as he described them and held the knife up for Melody to appreciate its full capacity.

"And the pouch will help to keep it safe. Perhaps I should have had it embossed with your initials..." Roman looked momentarily crest-fallen and boyish. It was not an emotion Melody had seen him display before and she was warmed by it. She held out her hand for the penknife and Roman passed it to her.

"It's a good weight. The blades are fine and sharp. But you don't have to buy me things."

"I know I don't have to, but I wanted to. Call it an early birthday present if you like. Or perhaps a late one. When is your birthday, Melody?"

She had told no one, not even Agnes, that her birthday had come and gone on the first day of April. Melody was now eighteen years old.

"Two weeks ago. The first."

"Then take it as a belated birthday present, please." He closed the blades back into the handle and put the penknife back into its box, then offered it again to Melody.

"Alright, thank you." There was a moment where they both held the box, their fingers overlapping.

Roman bent forward and kissed Melody's cheek, whispering "Happy birthday."

She felt colour come to her face and she swallowed.

"Your dinner will be getting cold." She took the box fully from him, with a shy smile.

He nodded once, his eyes lingering on her for a moment longer before he turned and strode out of the room.

Cook had been pleased to receive the new spoons from Melody, and had asked without shame if she could have some more.

"These are so much better than those bodged jobs I had from Robey last year. Split they did, as soon as they were in water!"

"Perhaps they used the wrong wood. I can make you some more. You'll want different sizes."

"Yes, and if you can put a hole in the end so I can hang them up, they'd be useful. Are your hands clean?"

"Of course they are, I've been reading to Mrs Cranshaw."

"Here you are then." Cook placed a plate of early potatoes and a thick pork chop on the table in front of Melody in the little staff dining room. "What's that you've got?"

Melody had put the box from Roman on the table as she sat down.

"A new penknife."

Cook picked it up without asking permission and opened the lid. She noted the silver hallmark and looked suspiciously at Melody.

"Where d'you get it?"

"Mister Roman gave it me. Said I was to have it as a birthday present."

"Did he, now. Fancy that. And after all the trouble you've caused too."

Melody was about to put one of the baby potatoes into her mouth but stopped. "What trouble?"

"All the arguments. Don't tell me you don't know as I shan't believe you. Almost every day those two brothers are bickering over something and always your name comes up."

Melody put her fork down on the plate. "I know they argue. Agnes tells me. But she never said it was about me. I don't want them arguing about me."

"Men will do more than argue if a pretty girl turns their heads. Eat your dinner. I've got enough to wash up this evening without waiting for your plate as well." Cook said over her shoulder as she disappeared back into the kitchen.

Melody looked at the food on the plate, the thick gravy dotted with grease from the chop. She had begun to feel at home on the Cranshaw's farm, but if she was the cause of discord between the brothers, could that threaten her peaceful routine?

The oil lamp swung in his hand as he climbed the style into the field. Holden Prentice had brought it to illuminate the unfamiliar ground as there was no moon that night.

He had not intended to stray from Emmett Green when he entered the Horseshoe inn that evening. He had gone in search of some local young men who he could tap for a free drink or two while telling some tall stories and perhaps winning a game of cards. He had found companions, but the conversation that evening was subdued and focused mainly on young women who did not appreciate the attentions of eligible bachelors. They were ungrateful, thinking themselves above their suitors. Someone mentioned that the group should simply not take no for an answer, and another said he had heard that in days gone by the bargees would kidnap young women from Emmett and sail them across the sea to Spain to sell them into slavery.

This talk brought Holden Prentice back to thoughts of Melody, and of how she had not seemed to be sufficiently punished for rebuffing his advances. He grew louder in his cups, and encouraged by his companions, declared he was going to demand satisfaction from the particular young lady who had spurned him. No names were mentioned; all of the group could have been discussing the same woman, but each had their own object of desire that evening.

Holden lurched out of the Horseshoe and headed towards the estate buildings. The barn doors were not locked or bolted. On the shelf just inside the door were the crank handles for the two small tractors used to pull the machinery to keep the lawns mown and other activities that the gamekeepers often observed as they took their lunch in their own hut. Next to the crank handles had stood the oil lamp. Holden picked it up, looked at it as if it were some mystical contraption, then hooked it onto the shaft behind the seat. A cat emerged from the space between the barn and a pile of bricks. It glanced at Holden with distain, then continued on its nightly vermin patrol.

Co-ordinating his limbs with the crank handle was a challenge. It continually fell out of its socket onto the barn floor. Sweat rolled down Holden's face as he made attempt after attempt to turn the crank handle. The tractor's engine turned over briefly, but by the time Holden had stood up, stopped swaying and gone around to the seat, the engine had died again. He took a swig from his hip flask, breathing hard. He replaced the cork stopper and having slid the flask back into his inside jacket pocket, grasped the crank handle again.

Cook's words troubled Melody. She had finished her dinner in silence and left quickly through the kitchen door, the penknife safely in its pouch inside her breakfast bundle. Though there were many objects in the drawing room that she was curious about, she still felt a sense of unease being in the solid farmhouse. The only things she touched while she was with Catherine Cranshaw were the books in the bookcase.

At least, that was all Melody was aware of touching. What she did not realise was how Catherine Cranshaw was becoming more aware of Melody's visits. She still paid little attention to anything else that happened around her, but for the hour or so while Melody sat with her and read or spoke of her day,

Catherine smiled and was at peace. That she mistook Melody for a companion of many years before did not matter to either of them.

There was a chill in the air as Melody reached the shepherd's hut. She decided not to sit outside that evening, though she left the door of the hut open. She broke some twigs and fed them into the little black stove, and set a can of water on top to boil for tea. She took off her boots and stood them by the door, lit her small lamp, then when the tea was made, she sat cross-legged on her bed and took out the penknife once again.

Melody could see that this knife had not been made with the purpose of rough work in mind. The blades were sharp but fine and would be better suited to taking flower cuttings for a lady's vase than stripping hazel rods or hacking away at brambles in a hedgerow. The nail file intrigued her. She understood what it was for; Cicely had something similar and would often work at shaping and smoothing her nails as they sat and talked in the wood. Melody had never used one herself as her nails were chewed short so as not to catch when she worked. She looked at her hands now: scratched and with freckles across the backs, the knuckles large and the nails half covered by their cuticles and dirty. She had washed her hands before seeing Mrs Cranshaw, but never thought to scrub them.

Closing the knives and leaving the nail file open, Melody began to dig carefully under each nail with the pointed end of the file. Some nails had nothing above where they joined her skin to dig under. When she had worked across both hands, finding it difficult to hold the nail file in her left, she looked at the detritus and winced. She should use the nail brush the next time she went to the farmhouse.

A thought occurred to her. What if Roman Cranshaw was trying to tell her he thought she was dirty? Melody blushed deep red despite being by herself in the hut. Many across the Vale said the woodlanders were unclean, often saying the same of the bargees and the showmen families. It was without merit; the woodlanders bathed regularly and the women kept their hair clean with a mixture of plant extracts and soapwort. What did Melody care if Roman took that much notice of her?! She was flattered, but it would have mattered so much more had Abbot Cranshaw commented on a grubby fingernail.

It had been some time since Holden had driven a vehicle, but once he had cranked the engine again and had it ticking over with its rhythmical pthut-pthut sound, he felt confident that he could manage the gears and brake. His first attempt resulted in stalling the engine. After much swearing, more cranking, and almost driving into the door frame of the barn, Holden maneuvred the tractor out across the cobbles and into the road. He was fortunate that the tractor's kerosene tank was full, but it took him some minutes to understand the gears alongside the clutch, having to remember not to depress the clutch so far that it became the brake.

Progress was slow along the road, but Holden had no intention of walking to the Cranshaw farm that night. He gave no consideration to the clanking and grinding of the tractor, or that it could run out of fuel. He was simply focused on confronting Melody.

Roman Cranshaw lay in his bed, his arms crossed above his head against the wooden headboard. Try as he might, he could not get Melody's face out of his thoughts. He was annoyed with his infatuation; that a nearly thirty-year old man could be so taken with such a young girl was ridiculous! And yet, what was thirty? He felt no older than he had when he sailed across the channel to Dieppe the first time in his army kit. No, that was not quite true, he reminded himself. He knew more, and felt more weary some days with the endless onslaught of ministry requirements than he had ever thought possible.

He also felt alone, he realised. Abbot was less interested in the running of the farm and never seemed to take his share of responsibility seriously. Roman knew if it were not for their mother being in her current state, Abbot would have left the farm and found some way to complete his legal training. Perhaps that was why he took less interest in the farm, Roman pondered. Or perhaps it was Abbot's experience of war that had led him to behave in a more care-free manner. That they had both returned when David had not, had affected them differently.

Roman brought his arms down and rolled onto one side facing the window. He had left the curtains open as usual and could see the feet of the constellation Ursa Major in the deep blue sky. If Abbot did leave, he would have no claim on the farm. Roman as the eldest surviving son held the inheritance. He deserved it, he decided as he slowly slipped into sleep. He deserved it all.

Holden Prentice was not so drunk that he did not realise the noise the tractor was making would alert the entire farm household to his presence. He turned into the lane that led to the farmhouse and further on to Robey, made several attempts at a circle so that the tractor was again facing the way he had come, then killed the engine. The silence was disorienting for a moment and he sat gripping the steering wheel while the vibrations left his body. Then he dismounted, took another sip from his hip flask and began the unsteady walk to the object of his still burning ire.

He passed the farmhouse and noted that all of the windows were in darkness. No burning the midnight oil for wealthy landowners! Holden snorted to himself, which became a cough that he hastily muffled with his sleeve. He stood still for a moment, suddenly fearful that the Cranshaws might also employ a gamekeeper or two. He detected no other sound or movement and relaxed, smiling to himself that perhaps they should and perhaps he should offer his services.

Holden walked on the grass to the side of the lane so that his footsteps could not be heard. He paid no attention to the silent barn owl that crossed his path only a few feet ahead of him, or the scurrying bank vole that ran for its life in the opposite direction. As he neared Ribble Top field, a Tawny owl cried out and was answered by its mate somewhere amongst the trees. The only thing out of place that night was Holden himself.

The field gate was closed. Holden fumbled with the catch and finally opened it, stepped through and let the gate gently bump closed against the post. He listened for a moment, taking another sip from his hip flask. Then, satisfied that if Melody was inside she must also be asleep, Holden crossed the pasture to the shepherd's hut steps.

In his bedroom, Abbot was sound asleep. He had written to James in his room after dinner that evening, mainly to avoid Roman's brooding, oppressive presence. The letter was full of Melody. A small mention of Isobel, but only to include her in thanking the family for their recent hospitality. Abbot had made up his mind to ask Melody to marry him, and wanted James to be his best man whenever a date was set. They would take a cottage somewhere, and have Catherine live with them if Melody agreed. Abbot felt certain that he was making the right decision for all of them: he was going to ask Melody in the morning.

Melody had been asleep for some time. She was also dreaming, but not the contented dream of one who was safe in their surroundings. She dreamed that she was back under the Fenny Bridge but this time she was alone. The river was running rapidly, lapping at her feet, and she could hear horses' hooves on the roadway above her head. She had a feeling that the horse carried someone who was looking for her and in her dream she pressed herself as close to the arched wall of the bridge as she could. She moved on her bed, bumping her elbow on the side of the hut, and began to wake up. It was then she heard the unmistakeable sounds of someone stumbling on the steps outside, swearing and then pulling at the hut's door.

Holden's foot had slipped on the wooden step as his shoes had picked up much moisture from the grass. He steadied himself, then fumbled around on the door to find the handle. He pulled at it, then turned it and pulled again. The door opened quickly, almost sending him flying backwards. He swayed precariously on the bottom step, pushed the door full open and ascended again.

Melody was awake now. She could only make out the shape of Holden Prentice silhouetted dark against the night outside. She had no idea who it was until he spoke.

"Melody Trow. Thought you'd get cosy on our doorstep, did you?"

Even as he slurred the words, his voice was unmistakeable. Melody began to pull herself up on the bed, squeezing herself into the corner while in that same moment realising that Holden was blocking her escape.

"Get out!" She shouted, her voice brittle. Melody could hear how pathetic it sounded, and Holden laughed as he took a step inside the hut, swaying and reaching out to steady himself against the wooden siding.

"Get out," he mimicked in a high voice. "Oh Holden, get out, leave me alone!" then his voice dropped back to its usual register, "What makes you think you can tell me what to do? Eh? No one will hear you this time."

Melody thought quickly. Staying on the bed was almost an invitation to Holden; she'd have a better chance to defend herself if she were standing up. Keeping her eyes on the now clearer though shadowed features of Holden, she slowly began to move her legs to the side of the platform.

"People come up and down this lane all the time." She hoped to keep his attention on her words and not her movements.

"Not at this time of night. Everyone else is tucked up in their beds."

Holden launched himself towards Melody just as she pushed herself up off the bed. He lashed out at her, wanting to inflict pain first and foremost. They came together, fists clenched and thrashing in the dark. Holden was off balance once again and tried to wrap his arms around Melody. She stumbled backwards, trying to turn the man so that he wouldn't pin her beneath him. They crashed into the back of the hut, with Melody's arm caught below Holden's embrace. Melody felt the floor of the hut shift; there was no time to wonder if the axel had broken underneath. She struggled, trying to bite Holden through his coat collar. He brought up his hand and punched at her, catching her on the forehead but without much force: there was no room to fully swing his arm in the cramped conditions.

He was strong because he was drunk. She was strong because she had worked physically all her life. They were matched in height, but Melody's advantage was her unclouded thoughts.

Now Holden began to twist Melody towards the bed. Her hand brushed the little stool and caught the penknife, spinning it. She scrabbled her fingers across the flat wooden surface while with her other hand pushing her palm upwards against Holden's nose and clawing at his eyes. She could smell the alcohol on him, his sweat was thick with it. He couldn't hold her still and fight her off at the same time. Holden relaxed his grip for a moment and Melody lunged at him again, bringing her fist up and driving the nail file end of the penknife into his bicep.

Holden screamed with pain and surprise. He let go completely of Melody and grabbed at the penknife sticking out of his arm. In the sudden movement he caught his foot and shin against the side of the platform. It sent him sprawling backwards with a thud.

It had been no more than two minutes since Melody had woken. She sank down until she was sitting on the edge of the bed, breathing hard, her heart pounding in her ears, her whole body trembling. Holden was on the floor, almost covering the whole of the available space between Melody and the door. She had to get out, but was he pretending so that he could grab at her again as she tried to step over him?

BESTED AGAIN

"HOLDEN? HOLDEN, GET UP."

Melody could only hear the sound of her own breathing. The man was on his side, his head near to the little black stove. Melody looked at him for a moment longer, then grabbed her pack from the corner of the hut. She had kept most of her few belongings inside it as there was little storage in the hut. Now she grabbed the few items that were in regular use, rolled up the blanket from the bed and shoved it into the top of her pack. Vernon's pack stood beside hers. It would have to stay behind; she had removed his few valuables and his tools were now in the top of her own pack.

She looked again at the body on the floor. Holden had not moved. Melody's boots were by the door. She quickly put on her dress and coat, wriggled into the shoulder straps of her pack, then carefully stepped around Holden. She did not do up her boots until she was down the steps and had reached the field gate. Then she tied the laces with still trembling fingers.

Out on the lane, Melody looked down towards Robey. She still wasn't sure where that road led, though she assumed it must either be to Derring or further south to the English Channel coast. She had no idea of the time, but there were no lights showing up at the farmhouse. She could pass by and take the Audling road, and be well away before anyone came looking for her. She set off, tears now threatening to spill over her lashes.

How had he found her? Why had he come and now spoiled everything all over again? If he were dead, they would blame her. They would come for her, no matter where she went. She would have to leave Wynn Vale; it wouldn't be safe for her to stay so close to the scene of her crime. By the time she reached the junction where Holden had left the tractor, Melody had convinced herself that she had killed him and could almost hear the bell of the police van and the whistles of the policemen as they hunted her across the countryside with their snarling dogs. She took one wistful look towards Emmett. She would probably never see it again now. Melody felt she would bring shame on everyone who knew her. Better to go where no one knew who she was or what she had done.

Clouds had covered the stars, and a while after turning towards Audling, Melody felt the first rain drops against her face. Tiredness swept over her. Would she gain anything by walking all night in the rain? Melody decided not. She could just make out Fenny Bridge in the distance and hurried towards it as the rain became heavier. The path down to the river was overgrown now with spring vegetation. Melody slipped and landed on her thigh, grazing her hands. Only her pack saved her from hitting her head, though it made it difficult for her to regain her footing. Eventually she made the bottom of the path, and huddled on the sandy soil under the bridge arch.

The river was not as high as she had dreamed, but it was higher than when she had last been there.

"What should I do?" she spoke quietly, but out loud. Not expecting to receive a reply, Melody took out her blanket and wrapped it around herself. Then she set her pack on its side, and laid down resting her head on it. She could feel a bruise where Holden's fist had caught her. She was not afraid of the dark; she was dry, there was a little food in her pack and water was available. If she had known the word, she would have described her feeling as stoic acceptance.

Melody did not immediately close her eyes. She listened to the rain falling against the plants by the bridge, and the rippling of the river as it passed by her, unconcerned that she was watching. Across the water on the far bank, a fox emerged through the reeds. It trotted to the abutment and after a small hesitation crept under the arch just as Melody had. She watched as the fox sniffed around on the sandy beach before turning in circles twice and finally settling down to see out the shower. It looked across at Melody as it tucked its nose under its tail. She would stay until the morning.

Abbot woke early feeling refreshed and optimistic. Today would be the day he took control of his future and broke out from under Roman's shadow. And David's; although he had never felt quite as competitive with his elder brother, he knew Roman had. Being the youngest had its advantages. He smiled at his reflection in his mirror as he shaved; yes, today would be a good day.

Abbot was about to go down for an early breakfast when he glanced out of his bedroom window. Smoke was rising from where he knew the shepherd's hut to be; a walnut tree obscured the view from his window but kept his room shaded in summer. It was too early for the hands to have been set to work for the day. It had to be Melody's hut!

Abbot raced down the stairs, out of the farmhouse and sprinted through the garden to Ribble Top field. He slowed as he approached the hut. Despite the overnight rain, it was well aflame, the wood crackling and sending orange sparks into the sky. If anyone were inside, they could not be saved now. As Abbot watched, the roof of the hut collapsed, sending a new shower of sparks and smoke upwards.

Holden Prentice stood by the field gate watching the flames. He had caught his head on the corner of the little stove as he fell at the end of his fight with Melody and had been knocked unconscious. When Holden came to, the effects of the alcohol of the night before had given him a raging thirst, and little memory of how he came to be in a shepherd's hut and not in his own bed at the Marchett Estate gatehouse. The penknife had come out of his arm during his fall, the nailfile breaking off from the main handle. It had caused him no lasting damage, but the entry site was red and sore.

She had done it again. Melody had got the better of him, this much he did remember, and was now nowhere to be seen. He didn't care where she had run to; he was going to make sure she couldn't return.

Unsteady on his feet still and with his head throbbing in time with his arm, Holden took a final sip from his hip flask and poured the remaining alcohol over the bedding that Melody had left behind. He remembered seeing a pile of twigs and sticks beneath the hut and brought some inside, laying them on top of the bedding. He kicked over the little stove, leaving the pipe chimney hanging from the roof. The coals were still warm, glowing faintly orange where they had been in the centre of the stove. Holden scattered them across the floor and used a couple of the sticks to lift some larger coals onto the bed. Then, to make absolutely sure, he went back out and collected a couple of handfuls of dry leaves that had not been wetted by the rain in the night, and used them as tinder along with some wood shavings to get a fire started.

When Holden was satisfied that the fire would not go out, he picked up the bucket of water that Melody had left at the end of the bed platform and went out. He closed the door, walked around to the back of the hut and used a branch to break the small window.

The activity had exhausted him. He set the bucket down and used his hands to scoop water up onto his face. He could hear the fire starting to take hold and smoke was beginning to emerge from the chimney and through the broken window. Pity Melody Trow wasn't inside, he thought as he kicked the bucket across the field towards the hedge. The violent movement made his head swim and for a moment he felt he might be sick. Cautiously, he walked past the hut and decided to watch while he leaned on the field gate and waited for his head to stop swimming.

Holden saw Abbot approaching before he himself was seen. Holden recognised him as the young man on the horse which Melody had led away the last time Holden had been in that field. As Abbot came closer, Holden marshalled his thoughts into what he felt would be a plausible excuse for his being there.

Abbot shouted to Holden, "You there! Do you know if anyone was inside?"

"No idea. I was taking an early walk and saw the smoke. Thought I'd see what was amiss. Nothing to be done now."

"And you haven't seen a young woman? About my height?"

"Haven't seen anyone but you." So, Melody was not at the farmhouse. She must have high-tailed it away while he was passed out on the floor. Perhaps she had learned her lesson now not to try and get the better of him.

The shepherd's hut suddenly fell into itself completely as the axels gave way to the flames. Two of the farm hands arrived up the lane from Robey, having run most of the way after seeing the smoke. Then Agnes could be heard shouting for Melody as she ran through the garden and across the field.

Abbot caught her as she tried to run past him, "She's not there! Agnes, she's not in there!"

"Oh my Lord, I saw the smoke from Mrs Cranshaw's room when I took in her tea. Where is Melody? She wouldn't do this, she loved being out here!"

Holden decided it was time for him to leave the scene of the crime. He was about to slip out through the gate when Abbot called to him.

"You said you were taking a morning walk. Where is it you are staying? I don't think I've seen you around here before."

"Not nearby. I'm taking a tractor back to Emmett, I left it up on the Audling road. I'd better be getting back with it – now I can see there's nothing to be done here." Holden gave a wave of his hand and began his walk back up the lane to where he thought he had left the tractor. His story didn't sound as plausible now that he had said it out loud, but no one could prove he'd had anything to do with the fire.

Abbot set the farm labourers to beating out any flames on the grass that threatened to get out of hand, and sent Agnes back to the house to see if Melody had made her way there along the road. He couldn't understand her absence; if she was anywhere close she would have seen the smoke and surely come running just as he had. Where was she?

Roman woke as Agnes brought a jug of warm water into his room. She sloshed some of the water onto the floor in her agitation over Melody's disappearance.

"Watch out! Are you shaking, Agnes? What's the matter with you?"

"I'm sorry Mister Roman, sir, I'll get a cloth."

"Has something happened? Are you ill? You're as white as a sheet." Roman sat up in bed, causing Agnes to blush at the sight of his bare chest.

"It's Melody, sir. Her little hut has burnt down, and no one knows where she's gone."

"What? How has it burnt?"

Agnes realised Roman was about to push the covers away and get out of bed. She hastily turned her back.

"I'll get that cloth." Agnes hurried from the room.

Roman did not need to stand up to see the smoke in the distance. He sat on the edge of his bed, hands on knees, staring in fascination at the remains of the shepherd's hut that now resembled a Halloween bonfire in its last throws of life. Surely the girl would not have set it alight herself? If it were an accident, she would have raised the alarm at the farmhouse and asked for help.

He stood up and crossed to the jug and basin. Having bathed the night before, he only needed a shave that morning. This he accomplished quickly, dressed and hurried down to the dining room to see if more information could be had.

When Holden reached the tractor, he was sweating heavily again. His head still pulsed with an alarming underwater sensation and he had a raging thirst that would have to be quenched at the first stream he came to on his way back to Emmett Green. The site on his arm where the nail file had pierced his skin still throbbed. Yet his mood was buoyant. Melody Trow would rue the day she crossed him. No one would get the better of Holden Prentice. They should have burnt down the old man Trow's cabin rather than pulling it to bits the day after they left. Holden would have enjoyed watching the flames consume it.

Now he would take the tractor back, hopefully without anyone asking any awkward questions of him, have a bath and then find some breakfast. It wasn't unusual for him to be out late, or very early; his mother would accept whatever he told her as the truth.

Holden found the crank handle where he'd left it, hanging on the rusting hinge of a stone gatepost that had long since lost its gate. He fixed it to the front of the tractor and gave it an experimental jerky turn. There was no response from the tractor engine, but an alarming one from Holden's stomach and his head felt as if it might explode. He winced at the pain behind his eyes and leaned against the tractor for a moment, trying to marshal his thoughts. He couldn't push the tractor home. He couldn't explain leaving it behind. He had to get it started.

Taking a deep breath and gritting his teeth, he took hold of the crank handle again. This time his grip was all wrong; the metal handle flew out of his grasp, continued on its rotation and smashed into Holden's hand on its return. In agony, Holden took a step backwards too quickly, tripped over his own feet and landed on his back in the lane. He forgot the pain in his head; now everything for concentrated on the damage to his hand. He managed to get to his knees before vomiting the night before's drink into the dirt.

Unsteadily he got to his feet and kicked at the tractor wheel in disgust and fury. There was nothing for it, he would have to walk back down to the farmhouse and see if anyone would help him get the blasted thing started.

Catherine was in the dining room with Agnes attending her. Roman bent to kiss his mother's head before taking his place at the table.

"Where is my brother?"

"Still out with the hands I think, sir. He fair raced down to Ribble Top when he saw the smoke. Cook has done some kedgeree if you'd like some this morning?"

Roman nodded to show he would and was helping himself to coffee when the jangle of the front doorbell sounded throughout the house. Roman frowned but continued with his drink while Agnes wiped her hands on her apron and went to answer the door. He could hear her talking to someone, Agnes' voice took on an air of self-importance when she was undertaking her official duties that he had always found absurd. Then he could hear a man's voice, though not what was being said.

"Excuse me, Mother," he said as he stood up and left the room. It was an automatic courtesy, Catherine never responded.

Left on her own in the dining room, Catherine Cranshaw gazed around the room as if she were a visitor. Her eyes came to rest on the plate in front of her which held a boiled egg in a china egg cup and thinly sliced white bread, buttered and cut into soldiers. Catherine kept her hands in her lap and waited as her mother had taught her to do.

Holden had looked around the yard hoping to find a boy or one of the older hands to help him. The stables were deserted. He had no option but to ring the main doorbell and see if anyone was at home. Agnes recognised him immediately, then noticed how he was holding his hand close to his chest. She wasn't sure of the man's position, but felt he should be invited at least as far as the entrance hall. She was about to return to the dining room to fetch Roman Cranshaw when he appeared in the hall to her right. He too recognised Holden Prentice.

"Well?" Roman stood tall in the dark hallway, despite the door being open and allowing the morning light to illuminate a rectangle of the floor.

"The … gentleman was asking if someone could help him start his tractor, sir." Agnes took a step backwards and kept her eyes on the floor. She was fairly sure the man was not a gentleman but was at a loss for another suitable way to address him.

Holden adopted a light-hearted air, "Yes, I pulled over at the top of your lane when I saw the smoke, and to be truthful I also needed to have a run out. When I got back and cranked it, the handle flew at me, and I don't think I can get it to start again. I thought one of your men could lend a hand." He tried to smile; it was not a natural expression for him.

Agnes blushed again at his extra information.

Roman indicated to the open door, "Shall we? Agnes, put something on the hotplate for me and go back to Mother."

The girl happily trotted off, while Roman followed Holden out into the yard, closing the door behind them.

"What are you doing this far from Emmett Green?" Roman asked as they crossed the yard together.

Holden was ready for the question. "We'd lent a tractor out; I'm bringing it back."

"You must have set out early."

They were about to enter the lane when Abbot arrived. He pulled up short as he saw Holden.

"I thought you had to get home?"

"Crank handle took me by surprise." Again, Holden tried to smile, holding up his wounded and swelling hand as proof.

"Have you two already met?" Roman frowned at his brother, feeling something was not as it should be.

Abbot had the same sense of mistrust towards the stranger. "He was at the fire when I got there. You've heard from Agnes no doubt?"

Roman's frown deepened. "What were you doing so far down the lane?"

"I saw the smoke; thought I'd take a look."

"Is Melody in the house?" Abbot was more concerned with finding her than what the man had been doing.

"No. But if you had come down the lane," he turned again to Holden, "surely you would have seen her?"

"I saw no one." Holden sensed the mood shift. His belligerence surfaced despite his need for their help, "She can take care of herself, her sort always do."

"How do you know? Do you know her?" Abbot took a step towards Holden.

"Yes, he knows Melody. He's from Emmett Green. And I don't think I believe his little story. What are you really doing on our land?" Roman loomed at his brother's side, his eyes boring into Holden's.

Holden took a step back. "I came to see the smoke, I told you! Now look, the quicker you help me get the tractor started, the sooner I'll be on my way."

Abbot now looked at his brother in surprise, "Who is he, then? How do you know him?"

"He's one of the gamekeepers on the Marchett Estate. I recognise him from the Hunt."

Abbot's brain worked at lightning speed. The pieces of Melody's story snapped into place for him, placing Holden firmly in the centre of her troubled exodus. His punch caught Holden completely by surprise when it connected with his cheek.

"You did it! You set the hut on fire! You could have killed her! What did you do to her? Where is she?" Abbot was not allowing Holden to answer, his punches now raining down onto the man who had fallen to the ground once more.

Holden tried to protect his head with his arms, allowing Abbot's blows to catch the puncture wound on his bicep. Roman, bewildered at his brother's sudden attack, grappled with Abbot and eventually pulled him to his feet. Abbot pointed his finger at Holden who was attempting to get up.

"If you've hurt her, I will find you and whip you to within an inch of your life, and then I will haul you to the authorities and see to it that you rot in jail!"

He shrugged off his brother's hands and stormed off across the yard and into the house.

Roman, unaware of the details, gave Holden a look of distain. Abbot must have a reason to have behaved so outrageously, but for now, Roman wanted the man off his land.

"Get up, man," he growled, stepping around Holden and setting off up the lane.

BACK TO THE FARM

ABBOT RAN UP THE stairs to his room. The water in his jug was cold, but he poured it into the large ceramic bowl on his dresser and plunged his face into it all the same. After a moment of oblivion, he brought his head out of the water and stood, clutching the edge of the dresser, dripping onto the floor and staring at his reflection in the mirror. His heart was still racing, and if he had lifted his hands, he knew they would be trembling with the adrenalin rush of combat.

He had to find Melody and make sure she was unharmed. None of the farmhands had seen her on their way up from Robey; they all knew her now and would have told him if they had noticed her even from a distance, perhaps crossing the fields.

If I were Melody, where would I go if I could not go back to Emmett? Abbot thought to himself. Then he picked up the hand towel and dried his face and neck. He raked a comb through his hair, gave his knuckles a cursory inspection, then went in search of some food for his saddlebag.

Roman and Holden eventually got the tractor started, mainly with Roman turning the crank handle and Holden adjusting the gas gauge. They did not engage in conversation beyond the necessary instructions for their endeavour. Once Holden was in the tractor seat and the engine ticking over satisfactorily, Roman stood up and handed him the crank.

"If you come this way again, I will not stop my brother exacting whatever justice he feels necessary."

They locked eyes for a moment, Holden refusing to acknowledge the warning. Roman stepped around the tractor and without a farewell, started on his journey back to the farmhouse.

Roman was concerned for Melody's well-being, though it was not in his nature to show it as emotionally as Abbot. Could they be sure that Melody had not been in the shepherd's hut when the fire was started? Having disposed of livestock carcases by incineration over the years, and having seen what an incendiary bomb could do to a human in France, Roman was well aware that the shepherd's hut fire would not generate enough heat to completely destroy a body. He had just decided that he would go straight to Ribble Top field and inspect the ashes himself, when Abbot appeared in the lane on his mare.

"I'm going to look for her!" Abbot shouted. The mare was excited to be out on an unexpected run and did not want to stop.

Roman raised his hand in acknowledgement as his brother passed him. It was not a new revelation to Roman that Abbot had also grown to care for the girl as he had. When Melody was safely back on the farm, Roman decided, he would ask her to marry him and claim his right as the older sibling.

It was still only a little after seven. Melody had no way of knowing that for certain, but she had woken needing to relieve her bladder and had the opportunity to study the sky above the bridge. At least the rain had stopped. Melody assembled a small fire and used the tin from her pack to heat a little water for tea. Her allowance from Cook was dwindling; she would have asked for more that lunchtime had she still been at the farm.

Melody shook herself. It did no good to dwell on past times. She would miss Agnes as she missed Cicely, but it would be better for everyone if she continued on the road. She had not fully decided that Audling would be her final destination. Melody knew there was a much larger country beyond Wynn Vale; the further she went, the less likely anyone would be to connect her to the events of the previous night.

The fox had gone, Melody presumed, once it had stopped raining. She listened to the river's gentle song and found herself gazing downstream towards the meeting of the tributary and the main river Wynn. Perhaps she could follow the stream's path and find the bargees. They would take her down to Wynnham, or perhaps further along the coast. Melody had never seen the sea. The woodlanders looked inland for their markets.

While she was wistfully considering the life of the bargees on their boats, she slowly became aware of the sound of hooves on the road above. The little fire had not been enough to give off smoke, and she hoped it was just a farmer out early on the road. The hooves stopped, and Melody held her breath. Surely the police would have been alerted by now; was this someone looking to capture her and claim a reward? She silently stood up and and clutched the billhook she had used to make the kindling for her fire.

Abbot tied the mare to a fencepost and looked at the grass growing to the side of the bridge. Someone had passed that way recently; he hoped it was Melody. With his head and one arm through the strap of the saddlebag, Abbot slithered down the overgrown path and peered around the abutment of the bridge.

Roman stood a few feet from the gently smoking pile of black and grey timber, the little black stove standing resolutely upright with its door open. He had sent the men on up to the house, satisfied than no stray sparks would reignite or cause more damage to the scorched ground. He was relieved to find no evidence of a body, both for the legal and administrative nightmare that would have ensued as much for the safety of Melody. But that still did not explain what had really happened or where the girl was now.

He was about to turn away, his stomach growling at the lack of breakfast that morning, when something caught his eye in the ash. Roman looked around for something to use as a grappling pole, and after a few moments pulled a branch from the long grass. Taking the thicker end in his hands, he prodded the thinner twiggy portion into the ashes carefully, not wanting to start the flames into life again. It took a couple of attempts but eventually Roman succeeded in pulling the lump of silver on to the grass.

He discarded the branch and tested the metal with the tips of his fingers. It was still hot; the silver had melted out of shape, but the steel blades that had been folded inside the casing had withstood the fire. Roman's gaze flowed across the rest of the remains. He picked up the branch again and began to spread out the ashes, looking for any other metal objects that could have survived. Half an hour later, Roman dropped the branch, wiped his face with his handkerchief, and set off back up the field to the house. Melody had not left her tools behind; she had intentionally left, but without his gift.

Melody stared at Abbot as he rounded the side of the bridge. Her stomach fluttered but was it with fear or elation?

"Melody..." Abbot took two steps forward so that he was under the arch of the bridge. "Melody, you're safe?"

Melody dropped the billhook and stumbled towards him. The concern in his voice and his out-stretched hand had dissolved all of Melody's distrust. Abbot took her into his arms and gently smoothed her hair as she sobbed into his shoulder. Two or three minutes passed before Melody lifted her head.

"Have you come to arrest me?"

"Arrest you? What on earth for?"

"Holden... he's dead." Her voice was barely a whisper.

Abbot shook his head slowly. "No, he is definitely alive. But I think you should tell me just exactly what has been going on."

They sat next to the fire; Melody wrapped again in her blanket despite Abbot feeding twigs and kindling into a steady flame. As there was only one mug, they shared the weak tea while Melody retold the events of the night before. Abbot was appalled at Holden's behaviour, then amazed at the spirit Melody had shown, and finally nodded with understanding at how she had thought Holden Prentice had suffered a fatal blow to the head.

"But he is not dead, though I should have happily inflicted the fatal blow myself!" Abbot said when Melody fell quiet at the end of her tale. He rubbed his knuckles and flexed his fist.

"No! No, then you would be hung for murder and I ... I should never forgive myself if you'd done it in my name."

They looked at each other as the moment stretched out between them.

"Will you come back with me?"

"I don't know ... if he comes back again..."

"You'll be safe in the house, he won't get in."

"I can't stay in your farmhouse, you know I don't feel right there."

"Well, you can't stay in the hut now." Abbot realised he had not told Melody about the fire, so intent he had been on hearing her story first. "It's gone."

"Gone where? I didn't think it could be moved."

"Not moved, gone. Burnt to the ground. I'm sorry Melody, I suspect Holden Prentice set it on fire when he realised you had escaped him."

Melody gasped and covered her mouth with her hand. Abbot could see from her eyes that she was upset all over again.

"There now, it was just an old hut. And you are safe, that's the important thing. But look here, you can't stay out in all weathers living under a bridge! What is it that you have against good old bricks and mortar?"

Melody twisted the corner of the blanket, trying to find the words to describe the oppressive feelings she experienced when inside any large building. When she had worked on the Summerton's farm and the other girls had been giddy with the luxury of a bedroom, even one shared with three others, Melody had been happy to sleep in the hay loft.

"It feels ... heavy on me. Crowded. I can't explain it. Wooden buildings feel lighter."

"It must be something to do with you woodlanders and the trees."

"I think so. None of us settle well in yonder houses." Melody was silent for a minute, "I don't know that my mother settled well anywhere."

"Audling is nothing but bricks and mortar. Derring is much the same. I don't know of any other place like Emmett; it's like stepping back in time there."

"I can't go back. I can't stay at your farm. What work do women do in towns?"

Abbot was taken aback by the question. The woodlanders kept themselves so far removed from the rest of the world, it occurred to him that Melody would not be safe out on her own, even with her physical strength. There was so much she didn't know; she would surely be taken advantage of. He had to convince her to return with him, though he recognised that now was not the time to propose marriage.

"Many work in factories. There isn't much call for parlour maids these days except in the largest houses, and unless you can cook, there isn't much about. I say, if you really can't stomach sleeping inside our house, how about we clear out the room above the stables for you? You could still do your work; we'll need more hurdles and I can't imagine you would ever run out of hedges to lay! What do you say?"

Melody didn't like the sound of factories. Cicely's brothers worked at the saw mills and Melody thought factories must be something similar, though she had never seen one. She let her gaze follow the river once more as she considered Abbot's suggestion.

"And for purely selfish reasons," Abbot continued, "I know Mother enjoys your company so much. And you can have as much sandpaper as you like if it keeps Cook happily in spoons!"

"What of Roman?"

"What of him?"

"He can't be happy that I've brought trouble with me."

"Don't worry about my brother. Now, shall we put this fire out and set off? I brought a little food with me just in case, but I'd rather have something fresh and hot, wouldn't you? And while your tea is welcome, I much prefer coffee." He smiled at her, hoping she would agree.

"I'll come."

Agnes sat at the kitchen table watching Cook roll out pastry for a pie lid.

"I've always said, they're strange folk from Emmett. Fancy wanting to sleep in a loft rather than a decent feather bed!" Cook flipped the edge of the pastry onto the rolling pin and laid it over the pie in one swift, practiced movement.

"I think it's rather romantic." Agnes rested her chin on her palm and sighed.

"You young girls! Nothing romantic about having rats in your unmentionables. It's not natural for a girl to be working in the fields like she does. I wouldn't be at all surprised if she's put some kind of spell on Mister Abbot. The way he moons about after her."

"You think she's a witch? Oh no, no I'm sure she's not like that. I think it's Mister Roman who's sweet on Melody anyway."

"If you ask me..." Cook finished trimming the excess pastry away and began crimping the edges of the pie together, "...they're both under her spell and nothing good will come of it. She wants to make her mind up one way or the other, and sharpish. You can roll those trimmings out for me if you've nothing better to do and we'll make some jam tarts."

Roman had been brooding over Melody's actions. By the time she had returned to the farm with Abbot, Roman was involved in a long telephone conversation with a clerk from the Ministry of Agriculture, Fisheries and Food. That conversation left him in a dark mood, which he attempted to soothe first with a large measure of whisky and then with a walk out to the sheep, steering clear of Ribble Top field. He could not understand why Melody would have left something so obviously valuable behind. He had thought, when she accepted the penknife in the drawing room, that she had appreciated its craftsmanship, and possibly the symbolism of his regard for her.

Roman recognised that Melody had not shown any forward behaviour or led him to believe that she was in love with him. Yet neither had she shied away or reacted with any hostility when he had kissed her. She was a thoroughly confusing and unusual young woman, and he could not fathom her actions. There was something about her lack of deference that he found attractive, though he could not put his finger on exactly why. He did not see Melody as an equal, and yet when he was in her company, he felt as if he were talking with someone of his own class.

He found himself standing on the headland, way beyond the boundary of the farm, looking out at the English Channel. The wind was strong and roared in his ears, momentarily taking him back to the hell-scape that had been France.

It all came back; the grotesque statuary of men caught and hanging like scarecrows in the yellow-green light of flare fire. The madness of that time; the stench, the mud, the hysteria of a young corporal who had to be knocked unconscious to stop him blowing up the whole trench. And then the return to England, the madness of his mother's muteness replacing the constant noise of battle which still raged in his dreams. Roman sank to his knees on that headland and screamed into the wind, caring not if anyone should see or hear him, until he had no more voice and his hands were full of the soil of home for which he had fought to defend.

It was only when he returned to the farm much later that day that Roman learned Melody had been installed in the stable loft. Over dinner, Abbot explained where he had found Melody and how he had convinced her to return with him. Roman listened without commenting, realising that Abbot was more up-beat and happy about the situation than there was any reason to be. Unless...

"You should consult me before making these decisions about who is permitted to stay here. You seem to have taken quite a shine to our guest."

"Well ... it was a spur of the moment thing, she is a nice girl, but that's another thing: Melody needs some funds. It hadn't occurred to me until today that she might be in need of anything more than food and shelter, but being a woman, well..." Abbot's face turned scarlet and he took a sip of water.

"Quite. What did you propose?"

"We talked about how her family made their living in the past, and Melody is such a skilled carver, she really only needs the materials to transform into useful objects so that she can sell them. You've seen the spoons that she made for Cook?"

Roman shook his head, "No."

"No, you don't venture into the kitchen much; they are very well made. I think Jessop's down in Robey would take a few to sell. Melody can spin and knit too. Really, there seems no end to what she can turn her hands to!" He was waving his knife around as he spoke, such was his animation.

"Don't you think it strange that she refuses to come into the house fully, even if only on a temporary basis?"

"Yes, yes I do, but she seems to feel rather claustrophobic about it. It's just not what she is used to I suppose."

"I expect she would get used to it in time. She might have to, one day." Roman watched his brother to see if that prompted any response.

Abbot simply turned red again. "She might," he conceded without any further elaboration.

Roman bristled. If anyone were going to bring Melody finally into the farmhouse, it should be him. But let her start her own little enterprise; if she could bring in enough to cover her keep, it would be one less thing for him to worry about.

That night Melody lay on her makeshift bed, listening to the sounds of the horses and the occasional scurry of rodents. The trees now in full leaf whispered gently in the breeze. A vixen barked some way off, perhaps to attract a mate, perhaps to proclaim her own territory. Melody was not sure that she had made the right choice to return to the farm. She liked Abbot Cranshaw a lot, he had a way of making her feel happy without really doing anything deliberate or contrived. She was reasonably sure that he liked her; why would he have bothered to track her down and be so keen to bring her back if he did not.

Melody rolled on to her side, causing a new waft of straw and horse scent to envelope her from the blankets she lay on. Roman Cranshaw was the problem. Roman with his questions that felt like a schoolmaster setting a test. Roman with his assumption that he could kiss her – not that Melody minded, but it was the principle of the thing! And Roman with his gift. Melody froze. She had not considered the penknife since she had fled from the shepherd's hut. It must have melted in the fire, or worse still, Holden Prentice must have taken it for himself.

How could she have been so careless? It was clearly an expensive gift, no matter how impractical it would have been for her. What if Roman asked her how she was getting along with it? Melody couldn't lie. She had never been able to; Avens and Vernon had always known immediately if she had ever tried, though Melody never understood how they knew, and always drummed into her that lying was not only wrong, but also pointless. A bad truth was always a hundred times better than a small lie, they had told her repeatedly.

Now she was closer to the farmhouse it would be difficult to avoid Roman. She would have to try and keep out of his way so he would have no opportunity to ask about the penknife, or anything else. Melody fell asleep eventually long past midnight, with an uncomfortable sense of fear at what Roman Cranshaw might do if he found out that she no longer had his gift.

A SETTLED SUMMER

"A PENNY EACH. I won't pay more, so don't ask." Amos Jessop placed the wooden spoon back onto the counter-top and folded his arms across his chest. A round, balding man of fifty-two years, he was the third generation of Jessops to stand behind the counter in the little village shop. They had grown from selling other people's junk and seasonal produce from their garden, to a general store that serviced the whole village of Robey and the surrounding farms and cottages.

Melody knew full well Jessop would sell the spoons for at least tuppence each, but he had the means and she, at least for the moment, did not. It had taken her two weeks to pluck up the courage to ask. Agnes had encouraged her, and put in a good word for her at Jessop's without Melody's knowledge.

"A penny each and you'll take them all."

Amos Jessop sniffed, calculating the cost and profit. "I will." He held out his hand for Melody to shake. She gripped it firmly, surprising him, then let go and turned her hand over for the coin.

"Young Agnes tells me you're staying up at Cranshaw's."

"I am."

"Just temporary, is it?"

"For now."

"And you're from Emmett."

"I am." Melody let her up-turned hand rest on the counter.

Amos Jessop rubbed his chin, thoughtfully. "I used to know one or two people from Emmett. Jack Oakridge, the Flowerdews. Your people."

"You knew my Granfer? Vernon Trow?"

"I did. Not well, but I was sorry to hear of his passing. I was away on business at the time. Yes, sorry I was."

"Thank you much."

"You make baskets, like those." He pointed to a stack of small woven baskets near the entrance to the shop.

"I can."

"Bring me ten, sixpence each."

Abbot was waiting for Melody outside the shop. They had spent much of each day in each other's company since the fire. He still had not felt the time was right to propose marriage but was content with their relationship as it currently was.

Seeing that Melody had emerged without the spoons she went in with, Abbot broke into a wide smile. It made him look much younger than his twenty-five years.

"He took them all?"

"For a penny each. They were worth more, but I suppose at least they are sold. He wants me to make some baskets next."

"That's excellent! I'm sure as soon as people see how skilled you are they will be flocking to buy them."

They began to walk back through the village towards the lane that led to the Cranshaw farm. The church stood on the left, just beyond the Bellows Inn, with the old forge in between them.

"I'm going to sit with Granfer for a while."

"Of course. Would you like me to come with you ... or wait for you at the gate?"

"No, you go on. Thank you for coming with me today."

Abbot wanted so much to take her in his arms and kiss her, to celebrate her success and comfort her while she stood by her grandfather's grave. Instead, he nodded his head and stepped back a pace.

"My pleasure. I'll ... see you back at the house."

Melody smiled and waited for him to continue on his way before she lifted the latch on the lychgate. The churchyard grass had recently been mown, the stripes still visible as Melody walked in as straight a line as the graves allowed towards Vernon Trow's resting place.

The Cranshaws had paid for the funeral but had not purchased a headstone. A simple wooden cross painted white marked Vernon's grave. It was to the south of the church, tucked in a corner and surrounded on two sides with holly and hazel trees. Melody had no flowers, but Vernon would not have wanted any. She sat cross-legged on the grass at the foot of the grave, and closed her eyes.

Roman Cranshaw had decided to ignore Melody's new proximity. He had also largely ignored Abbot's lightness of mood, by taking his meals at odd hours much to Cook's annoyance.

Roman had more than enough on his mind with the farm, and had travelled to Audling to finally buy a new ram at the market. He was also accumulating as much literature from the Forestry Commission as he could with a view to taking advantage of their management scheme.

It was by accident rather than design that when Melody returned from Robey that afternoon, Roman was also in the stable yard, his head under the bonnet of their own tractor. There was no way Melody could gain entry to the stable without passing Roman, and at that same moment he stood upright and looked straight at her. There were more than thirty feet between them, yet to them both it felt more like three.

Roman reached for the rag on the tractor seat and wiped his hands. There it was again, that visceral need he felt to capture the girl, to keep her close.

Melody had stopped abruptly when she first saw Roman, but now clenched her fists and began to stride with purpose across the farmyard.

"I have something of yours." Roman's voice was harsher than he intended.

Melody stopped, colour rising in her cheeks. There was no avoiding the confrontation now. She relaxed her hands and looked down at the cobbles, but said nothing.

"You left it behind when you ran away. That was rather ungrateful, don't you think?"

Melody raised her head.

"I didn't think. I just had to leave."

"And yet now you are here. Again. Making good use of my brother's hospitality, again."

"I'm still working on the hedges. And I'll be able to pay for my keep. Here," she opened the purse that hung from her belt and scooped out a handful of pennies, offering them to Roman.

"Put them away, I'm not interested in your coin. What do you want from us, Melody?"

She was confused. The pennies trickled back into the purse and she let it drop back against her hip. What did she want? It was such a strange question to ask. For so long she had lived in the moment. Melody had never made plans or had dreams of this future or that. The future, she had learned, was unreliable. If the moment was uncomfortable, she might consider the next step to achieve a more pleasant situation, but only as far as that. She existed: she worked, ate and slept, and sometimes she sat with Catherine Cranshaw. She had never considered she might need to want more.

Roman took her silence as defiance.

"The least you can do is apologise! That penknife was worth a considerable amount. Anyone else would have taken it, even if they had meant to sell it or pawn it somewhere. But you left it as if it meant nothing at all!"

Melody heard the distress in his voice. She slowly walked forwards, so that they no longer had to speak so loudly.

"I thought I had killed Holden Prentice. With your penknife. It was stuck in his arm as he fell. All I could think of was to get away. I didn't leave it on purpose. I'm sorry you think I did."

Roman's anguish had a strange effect on her, almost as if she was breathing in his sorrows and finding them amplified in her own. Tears formed quickly and spilled onto her cheeks. She reached out a hand to touch his arm, and at the same moment he stepped forward and pulled her to him in an embrace that made her think of a man drowning at sea. Roman clung to her, not crying himself, but caught in a maelstrom of emotion where he could not distinguish between love and hate.

They stood for several moments, supporting each other silently. A squabble of sparrows landed on the cobbles, scratched around for a few seconds, then as the couple moved apart, took off again in formation. Roman held on to Melody's arms.

"I think ... No, I'm sorry. I have to ..." He let go and without looking at her again, fled across the yard and into the house.

Melody felt drained. She went around the tractor and into the stables, and climbed the ladder to the loft. Collapsing onto her bed of blankets and straw bales, she closed her eyes and thought she could still feel Roman's arms around her. Melody drifted off to sleep. She dreamed of her grandmother Avens setting out a tray of small cakes to cool. Each cake looked different from the others: some had fruit, some were plain but were more or less evenly browned by the oven. Melody was eight or nine in her dream. Avens looked at her with such devotion in her face, Melody felt loved and secure.

"Choose wisely," Avens said. "They're not all for you."

Melody woke with a start. She had only been asleep for half an hour; the sun was still above the farmhouse roof. Its light streamed through the tiny window of the loft, casting a beam through which spider silk and dust danced their endless waltz. It picked out a rectangle of gold at the top of the ladder on the oak beamed floor of the loft, and in its centre there now sat a lump of tarnished silver.

The summer drew onwards. Fruit began to swell on the trees, fields that had been sown turned green then golden, the wind rippling across them in waves. The lanes grew dusty and overgrown with tall grasses and brambles. Sheep were shorn, lambs and calves sold, pigs fattened, and chickens left to scratch over allotments that had finished their part in the productive cycle.

Melody had made every effort to avoid both of the Cranshaw brothers as much as she could. She missed Abbot's company, and occasionally found herself remembering Roman's embrace, but for much of her waking hours, she occupied herself away from the farmhouse and stables. Two or three afternoons each week she still spent with Catherine Cranshaw, in the drawing room. Roman and Abbot had never intruded on this time, and even Agnes was reluctant to interrupt Melody's reading aloud or her one-sided conversation with the older woman.

Melody continued to take her evening meal in the kitchen with Cook or in the servant's dining room. Agnes was usually waiting on the Cranshaws while Melody ate; it was easy for Melody to plan around their movements. Cook tolerated Melody in the kitchen, but did nothing to encourage her to linger after her meal. She would boil Melody an egg to take for her breakfast, along with a chunk of bread, another of cheese, and once a week Cook left her a small amount of tea in an envelope on the mantlepiece of the servant's dining room. Melody had begun to leave a few coins in exchange, when she had them.

There was no stove in the stable loft. Melody knew that before the winter she would need to find warmer clothes or warmer accommodation, but as July became August, she took her tools and supplies out to the woodland beyond Ribble Top field at dawn and stayed there until the sun told her it was dinner time. She had cried when she first saw the blackened wreck of the shepherd's hut, but her tears dried quickly as the rook she had befriended flapped down to inspect the fire site with her. Now she looked for the bird every day, and he seemed content to patrol the field some way off from her on the edge of the woodland as she carved or wove baskets in the shade of the trees.

It was because she spent so much time away from the farmhouse, that she did not hear the Cranshaw brothers as they bickered and argued. Cook had not mentioned it again; she was a loyal servant to the Cranshaw family and knew her place as well as how to hold her tongue when it mattered. Agnes felt the tension at mealtimes, but the brothers were also conscious of her presence. They restricted their comments to matters of national and international news, rather than those closer to home. Catherine Cranshaw did not deviate from her routine of silently waiting to be told to eat, once her food had been sufficiently cooled and cut up for her.

On her Wednesday afternoons off, Agnes sought out Melody as she walked down the lane to Robey. They would sit and talk, or if Melody had goods to sell to Jessop's they would carry them down to the village together. Agnes was being courted by a young man, an apprentice butcher, from the far side of Robey. They had met at a recital in the village one Wednesday evening; John Stoneham had walked Agnes back to the cottage she stayed at on her evening off. It was only a few hundred yards, but many appreciative glances were exchanged on that walk, and now John took his Wednesday supper with Agnes in the tiny kitchen of the cottage, under the watchful eye of the owner, Mrs Pennard.

When Agnes found Melody in her usual spot, she was red in the face from the heat of the August sun, despite her straw hat.

"Are you alright? Here, sit you down and have some water." Melody dipped her mug into the half-full pail and offered it to Agnes.

"It's a relief to be out of the farm, that's for certain! At it like hammer and tongs they've been all day." Agnes gulped down the water, dribbling a little on the front of her dress. She brushed at it with her fingers, "It'll dry quick enough in this heat."

"You mean the Cranshaws?"

"Yes. Every little thing sets one or the other off at the moment."

"So Abbot is back then."

"Came back late last night. Mister Roman wasn't happy that he'd stayed away longer than he'd planned. And then he turns up with his friends, wanting to have a party as late as it was."

"I saw the motor car in the yard this morning." Melody had assumed it belonged to a friend of Roman's and thought no more of it as she crossed the cobbled yard at just after six that morning.

"Such a mess they left in the drawing room for me to clear up, I can tell you! Cook's in a right state too, we've had to send Jim down to get more groceries to feed them all."

"How many are there?"

"Five extra to feed and water, and there's beds to make, baths to run, trays to take up and down the stairs... just as well it's summer, else I'd have the fires to make up and keep going too!"

Agnes' indignation made Melody smile despite feeling sympathy for her friend.

"The men are just men, but the women want everything done yesterday. Complaining last night that we had no ice. Complaining this morning that the bacon was too salty and the coffee too weak. They have some nice frocks though."

"Well you won't have to see them all tonight at least."

"Oh, I will! I've got to be back at the house by six so they can have their dinner before even more of them turn up. That set Mister Roman off as well this morning, when Mister Abbot told him. Cook asked me to tell you that you're needed in the kitchen to help her. They won't want you in the dining room, that's my job," she said as she swelled with self-importance, "but Cook says you're to come back with me later and help her with the washing up."

"I can do that. As long as they don't want me in one of those black frocks and pinnies you wear."

"Mine wouldn't fit you." Now it was Agnes' turn to smile. Melody was taller and a few inches larger all around than Agnes.

"Anyway, I can't sit here gossiping all afternoon, I need to let Mrs Pennard know I won't want any dinner, and ask her to tell Johnnie where I am. I'll shout for you on my way back up, alright?"

Melody listened to Agnes crashing her way through the undergrowth back to the lane. Archer the rook had flown off at Agnes' arrival, but now flapped lazily back to the field and resumed his patrol with one eye on Melody just in case she had any tasty morsels to offer him.

"Maybe I can bring you some treats tomorrow, Archer," she said out loud to the bird.

It was not in Melody's nature to be captivated by fashion or the goings on of town and gown. Agnes would sometimes share a magazine with her, cooing over the latest styles advertised or the hairstyles of famous actresses, while Melody tried to show some interest. But the news that Abbot had returned from his visit to his friends had given Melody a familiar turn in her stomach. She knew she should not refuse to help Cook; though Melody lived simply, she was well aware that it was only because of the Cranshaw's benevolence that she could do so and come and go as she pleased.

She picked up the half-finished basket that was at her feet, a small one suitable for use around a garden for cut flowers. Jessop had asked her to make two or three since he had been asked by a new-comer to the village for one recently. Several of the houses in Robey were now taken on six-month rental terms, by a variety of couples and single women. They added a colourful and often noisy summer interest to the villagers' conversations.

Melody wondered what Abbot's friends were like. He had spoken of James several times to her but never in great detail. Once again a feeling of the world stretching out beyond Wynn Vale washed over Melody. Perhaps, she though as her fingers mechanically twisted the soft willow withies into shape, she ought not to have returned to the Cranshaws' farm, but kept going in search of whatever lay along the road.

Two Worlds Collide

Abbot had been surprised to receive another invitation from James so soon after his previous stay. James and Isobel's parents were touring Mesopotamia over the summer: the siblings had decided to invite all of their friends to come and go as they pleased over the six-week period of parental liberation. It would be an opportunity to meet new people, James had written.

That had appealed to Abbot, as James hoped it would. It had become clear to Abbot that Melody was avoiding him. She was gone from the stable loft most mornings before Abbot had finished his breakfast, and rarely returned to the house for her supper before dusk. Though it pained him to think he had perhaps upset her in some way, he was conscious that his thoughts of marriage had been premature. Indeed, the notion now of restraining Melody in any way had become anathema to him. He understood that she was a free spirit, someone for whom society's standards held little meaning.

Yet he loved her still. That was undeniable and had caused him many nights of absent and broken sleep. He had turned to physical exercise, working in the kitchen garden and clearing ditches with the farm hands. It had toned his muscles but had not removed Melody from his thoughts. With the arrival of James' invitation, Abbot felt it could at least provide some temporary distraction from his current inability to concentrate on farm business. He wrote a short reply on the same day and within a week he has on his way to Pilton House for what he hoped would be an exciting and sociable stay.

With friends made in the army as well as at school, James' visitors were many. Added to those were Isobel's friends and acquaintances, some of whom also brought their friends. The bedrooms were full, and some were reduced to sleeping on sofas and armchairs. On one night, two hammocks were erected in the garden to contain extra guests so that they would not have to leave the party. It was a maelstrom of arrivals and departures, with motor cars and one or two motorcycles filling the gravel driveway.

Days were spent walking around the garden, which covered two acres and contained a stand of fir trees some way from the house where a small summerhouse looked out across countryside beyond while remaining in the cool shade. Other activities included walking to the nearest village to play bowls and tennis, or to swim in the river that passed through James' parent's garden. Some friends played cards, sketched, or simply sat around smoking and drinking endless pots of tea and cocktails. They were a gay assembly, where no one mentioned their war time experiences or commented on the unrest that was still an undercurrent across the country after the previous year's General Strike.

Abbot drank more than he had in a long while, slept late and some nights never made it into a bed at all. He felt this was what life should be about, enjoying everything it had to offer with people he only vaguely knew but who were exciting and held his interest with conversations on topics from fishing in the Scottish highlands to the divorce of a famous actor in Paris. It was through several of these conversations that a germ of an idea began to grow in his mind, that he might return to his original plan of becoming a lawyer. It would mean going away to university, then obtaining a pupillage, but once his studies were completed he would have a career to be proud of. One of the other house guests had just taken his final examinations and Abbot spent several afternoons in discussion with him.

Isobel had been excited to have one more opportunity to convince Abbot that she would make the perfect wife for him. All of her friends were now either married or engaged to extremely well-regarded men and Isobel was beginning to feel time slipping through her fingers. She had had a small number of offers, from men whom she considered to be either too old, too young, or too scarred by the war to entertain seriously. She wanted Abbot, and when a throw-away comment by one of her friends about never having seen truly rural life floated past her ears, she seized upon it.

"Abbot has a farmhouse way down on the coast, perhaps we should pay a visit?" Isobel fluttered her eyelashes slightly in Abbot's direction.

Abbot was at that point several pink gins into the evening.

"You would be most welcome! The old place could do with livening up a bit."

"We could take your motor car, Charles. I'm sure if we left now, we would be there before midnight. Oh, do say you'll drive, darling!"

And so, late that night, Charles' large motor car had brought Abbot home, accompanied by four others from Pilton House, Isobel among them. James had declined the invitation, feeling that he should not leave their remaining guests entirely without a host. The group had taken turns to drive, swapping seats in the car each time they had to pull over and wait for the engine to cool down on the rolling hills of northern Wynn Vale.

The following morning it had been Abbot's job to explain to Cook that there would be eight for dinner that evening and apologise for the short notice. Cook was not impressed, but drew on her years of experience and quickly dispatched one of the older farm hands to gather supplies. Roman had slept through his brother's arrival the night before. He finished his breakfast and shut himself in the study making it clear he was not to be disturbed.

Abbot made the wise decision to take his new friends out on a hike to take in an interesting church and two villages south of Robey. They were to picnic on the coast and then make their way back in the afternoon. If the exercise proved too much for them all, the bus from Derring to Audling would provide an alternative return route. As they all trooped past the woodland at the end of the Cranshaw's property, Abbot glanced into the trees regularly, hoping to see Melody. He was disappointed but was quickly distracted again by Isobel asking the names of various plants as they passed.

They had a pleasant day; the sun was bright and warm with just a few high clouds. The girls took off their shoes and stockings to paddle in the sea with squeals of delight. The men skimmed flat stones across the waves and lamented the absence of any small sailing boat that could have been hired for an hour. All agreed that as far as rural England went, the county of Wynn Vale was a particularly bucolic example.

Melody was waiting for Agnes on the edge of the wood at what she thought was about half past five. She sat on a fallen tree trunk, her tools in one of the baskets and the bucket now only containing her enamel mug at her feet. Agnes came up not long after Melody had sat down, and the two of them followed the lane to the farmhouse, entering through the kitchen door as usual.

Cook had been hard at work for hours, muttering to herself as she chopped, skinned, shredded and mixed. Provisions had been arriving all afternoon, and with Agnes absent, Cook had been forced to keep interrupting her preparations to receive them.

"At last! Now I might have a few minutes to take a cup of tea and a sandwich before I start on that lot." She waved a paring knife in the direction of a sheaf of carrots.

Agnes went straight up to her room to change back into her uniform, leaving Melody in the kitchen with Cook.

"Where do you want me to start?" Melody peered into the large sink to see if there was any water already there to start washing the pots and pans piled up to one side of it.

"You'll have to put a pan on the stove for hot water. Those girls have used all we had on their baths. On a Wednesday too! I've told Mister Roman we'll have Mrs Cranshaw's dinner ready at half past six so that Agnes can get her up to bed and out of the way before everyone else sits down. The rest will be eating at half past seven. You can put two pans on the stove, no doubt they'll be wanting more hot water for their tea." She sat down heavily on one of the kitchen chairs and took out a handkerchief to wipe her red, glistening face.

Melody did as she was instructed. Between sips of tea, Cook gave Melody a long list of actions to perform, and Melody knew they would have to be completed in the exact order Cook had spoken them to avoid the older woman's wrath. She set about them with a smile; she was used to Cook's grumbles and replied at strategic points with "yes" and "no" as appropriate.

With all of the windows open, the sounds of music came to those in the kitchen as Agnes brought in Catherine Cranshaw's empty plate and cutlery.

"I'll have the devil of a job getting the Missus up to bed with that racket going on."

"It's a good thing there's no near neighbours." Cook was whisking egg whites, and had been tapping her foot to the beat of the music not thirty seconds before Agnes came in.

"I can help you with her." Melody had just emptied another bucketful of peelings onto the compost heap in the kitchen garden, and had also lingered for a few moments to listen to the music. She knew what gramophones were but had never seen one working or playing the heavy, flat, black discs. She could also hear the laughter of the guests and her curiosity was piqued.

Cook nodded her consent. Melody followed Agnes along to the dining room where Catherine was still sitting at the table.

"It's just as well she's not a wanderer. Being like a baby is bad enough," Agnes whispered as they entered the room.

"Hello, Mrs Cranshaw," Melody said gently, moving to the far side of the woman in case she was needed to steady her by the elbow.

Catherine Cranshaw looked up at Melody and smiled, "Rosemary." It was the only word she had ever spoken to Melody in all the weeks they had been spending time together. Melody had never corrected her, never asked who Rosemary might be, and never reacted in any way to suggest to Catherine that she was wrong.

"Come on now Missus C, let's get you upstairs for your wash and bed. Perhaps Mel ... Rosemary," Agnes glanced at Melody over Catherine's head, "will read to you in your room today?"

"Of course. Let me move the chair."

They manoeuvred the woman out of the dining room, into the hall and up the stairs. Agnes steered them into the bathroom and began to run some water into the sink. She frowned as it remained cold.

"Cook said they've used all the hot. I'll go and get a jug from the kitchen." Melody was closest to the door and didn't feel she should linger during Catherine Cranshaw's ablutions.

She hurried down the staircase and as she turned towards the rear passage to the kitchen, she caught sight of the open drawing room door. Abbot was dancing with a young, slender woman whose head was thrown back in a hearty laugh. He too laughed and shook his head as they spun away out of sight. Melody frowned, then scolded herself. It was no business of hers who Abbot Cranshaw danced with. Those were his friends after all.

Melody's return from the kitchen was interrupted by Roman, who chose that same moment to emerge from the study and almost crash into her. The hot water slopped over the side of the jug and down Melody's front, making her swear.

"That's not language I expect to hear in here!"

"The water's hot."

"Are you burned? I didn't realise..."

"No, it just made me jump, you coming out like that."

Another peel of laugher came from the drawing room. Roman grimaced and ran his hand through his hair.

"I'd better get this up to Agnes." Melody wanted to ask Roman how he was, but the look on his face did not invite conversation. She turned before he could respond and carefully climbed the stairs.

Once Catherine was washed and in her nightdress, the girls led her to her bedroom which thankfully, as Agnes observed, was over the kitchen with a window that looked out across the far side of the house and the kitchen garden. The music could still be heard, but not loud enough to prevent sleep. Agnes drew the thin curtains across the open window, despite the sun still being above the treetops. It cast a pink glow around the room through the fabric.

"You all right to read to her now? I need to start taking the first course through." Agnes was noticeably nervous at waiting on a larger party than she was used to.

Melody looked around for a book, then realised where she had left it the last time she had sat with Catherine.

"Her book's in the drawing room." She took a deep breath. "I'll go and get it and then you can do your serving."

She did not want to go into the drawing room. Her unfashionable outfit suddenly became a collection of old rags in her eyes. At least she had not worn her trousers that day, knowing it would be hot in the afternoon. When she reached the bottom of the stairs, she paused for a moment in front of the large mirror that hung in the hallway. Her sun-browned face with golden highlights in her hair stared back at her. She pulled the wooden dowl from the piece of leather she used to keep her hair tied back, and retwisted her locks before reapplying the dowl to the leather. As she lowered her arms, Roman's face showed in the mirror. He was standing on the other side of the hall.

Melody spun around. "I need to get your mother's book from the drawing room." She began to walk towards the now closed door.

"I'll come with you. Cook asked me to have everyone assemble for dinner."

They reached the drawing room door together and stopped. Roman lifted his hand to tuck an escaped strand of Melody's hair behind her ear.

"I have missed seeing you." He said quietly.

"I thought you were busy."

Roman gave a rye smile, "I have tried to be."

A cough sounded behind them. Cook was carrying a large tureen of soup into the dining room, her hands wrapped in cotton tea towels.

Melody grasped the door handle and marched into the drawing room. Ignoring the stares of the house guests, she walked straight to the small side table by the window and picked up the little blue hardcover book. She intended to march straight back out again without making eye contact with anyone. She had not bargained for Isobel.

"Good heavens, Abbot, you never told us you had a little sister!"

They had stopped dancing. Everyone was looking at Melody who had frozen at the sound of Isobel's voice, while Roman stood just inside the doorway. Melody felt her face begin to burn.

"No, no, I have no sister! That's just Melody. Come and say hello, Melody!" Abbot's face was flushed with the exertion of dancing and the effects of their pre-dinner cocktails.

Melody held the book to her chest and turned slowly. She saw each of the strangers as exotic birds, all appraising her and if she were not family, immediately relegating her to the realms of 'staff'.

Isobel clutched Abbot's arm and giggled. "Rather the gypsy! You were right, Eliza, the modern styles take so long to reach these far-flung corners of England."

The other woman, Eliza, giggled to echo her friend. Roman stepped forward.

"Dinner is about to be served, if you would all come this way?"

"Are you dining with us Melody?" Isobel fluttered her eyelashes innocently.

"No, I..."

"Melody prefers to eat by herself." Abbot could have kicked himself as the words came out. They sounded like a snide reprimand, rather than a statement of fact.

"So would I, if I had to wear those clothes," Eliza giggled once more. "Come along Charles, walk me in, I could eat a horse!" She grasped Charles' arm and began to drag him towards the door.

Melody's lip began to tremble. She looked at Abbot and Isobel standing so closely together, then fled from the room. Roman started to reach out to her as she passed him, but the look on her face warned him to let her escape. He could not tell if it were anger or embarrassment but recognised her need to flee.

Melody raced up the stairs and into Catherine Cranshaw's bedroom, where she was met again with upturned faces. This time they were friendly; Melody forced a smile and waved Agnes away as she asked if everything was alright. She took up the seat next to the bed where Catherine now lay propped up on several pillows, and opened the book where the bookmark had been placed. She cleared her throat, slowed her breathing with some difficulty, and began to read aloud.

Around the dinner table, the guests chattered on, oblivious of the drama they had just witnessed. Roman sat at the head of the table, refusing to meet anyone's eyes and only responding monosyllabically to any question asked of him. He excused himself before dessert, shooting a hostile glance at his brother who did not notice it.

Abbot sat toying with his food. How stupid he had been, to think for one moment that Melody might fit in with his usual crowd. She was head and shoulders above them all, in her looks, her manner, her accomplishments! The constant giggling of Isobel and Eliza began to grate on his nerves as they moved from the main course to dessert. Isobel's thinly veiled criticisms of his family home, Cook's meal, the weather and lack of alcoholic options grew in his mind from pin pricks to daggers. How had he not noticed her lack of sensitivity before?

Yet Abbot was still their host, and over the fruit crumble and custard, he attempted to pull himself out of his morose state. By the end of the meal, he had agreed whole-heartedly that the full extent of entertainment in Wynn Vale had been exhausted in just one day and that rural life, though pleasant enough, did not suit everyone's tastes.

"Perhaps it would be better to return to Pilton House and take up the tennis again?" Charles mused aloud.

"Oh, we can't leave Abbot, we've only just arrived!" Isobel failed to disguise the note of panic in her voice.

"No, really, I agree with Charles. It has been perfectly delightful to have you all here, but I think my brother feels I have been neglecting my duties on the farm and I can always come up again in a few weeks, Isobel." Abbot decided in that moment that he would write and explain everything to James, if only to avoid another close encounter with his sister so soon.

"We'll set off after breakfast. I'm sure we'll manage with one less driver, as long as Eliza doesn't get us stuck behind another herd of cows!" Charles laughed.

"That was hardly my fault, they simply appeared out of nowhere. Shall we leave the men to their port, Issie?"

Abbot pushed his empty bowl a little further away from him and placed his napkin on the table.

"No need, girls. We're not quite of that class here. Let's all go back to the drawing room and see if we can find the playing cards. I'm in the mood for Bridge." The last thing he wanted was for the two women to wander off in search of Melody.

BROTHERS COME TO BLOWS

CATHERINE CRANSHAW HAD FALLEN asleep to the sound of Melody's voice. The small china clock on the bedside table said twenty minutes to nine and Melody was hungry. She slid the bookmark between the pages, closed the book and put it silently on the table. She wondered if she should rearrange the bedding so that Catherine's hands were covered, but decided to leave things as they were. If older woman woke again, it could be hours before Melody could have her own supper.

Catherine looked at peace with her head turned to face the window, eyes closed and mouth slightly open. Melody could see Abbot in her face, but knew also that when Catherine was agitated, Roman showed in her features. When Melody had been a child, she had played at families with Cicely and some of the other wood children, but it had been a long time since she had considered ever having a child of her own. Standing in the warm bedroom, watching Catherine Cranshaw sleep, Melody wondered what a child of her own might look like. She had been told that she resembled her mother, but what was there of her father in her? Was he the reason she preferred to be by herself? Had he passed on some ability that lay as yet undiscovered?

Melody left the bedroom, closing the door as quietly as she could. She stood on the landing for a moment listening to the sounds on the ground floor and trying to determine whether she could get to the kitchen without bumping into anyone else. Roman's bedroom door was closed; Melody hoped he was inside. The music came again from the drawing room but quieter now. Melody decided to make her bid for her supper and trotted down the staircase.

Cook was not in a good mood. Abbot had told Agnes that the party would be leaving after breakfast, and when Agnes passed on the news to Cook, she wished she had not been the bearer.

"Tomorrow? After we've got all this extra food in for them thinking they'd be here until at least the weekend? What am I meant to do with it all, I'd like to know?! There's only so much bottling and drying I can do. And there's no good Mister Roman complaining about the accounts at the end of the month either. I shall tell him to look elsewhere! These young people, no idea what food costs these days. You needn't think you and the other miss will be eating it all, either!"

Agnes had been slowly shuffling towards the door, hoping to escape back to the dining room for the next round of dirty crockery.

"We could have some, if it's going to spoil otherwise. Melody never eats much anyway, I don't know how she manages on what she gets here. I'm always hungry."

"I shall have to redo the menus for the rest of the week. As if I didn't have enough to do. Here, don't leave those plates on the table. Where is that girl? She's meant to be helping in here!"

"She's reading to the Missus. I expect she'll be down in ... oh, here she is!" Agnes took the opportunity to scurry away.

Melody looked at the tower of dirty pots, pans and crockery and began to roll up her sleeves.

"Your supper is in there. It's likely cold now, but see you eat it before you start on those. Don't want you fainting on the job." Cook had lost some of her temper having sounded off at Agnes. She looked Melody up and down and pursed her lips.

"Agnes is right. You don't eat enough. You've lost weight since you came to us. See that dress is hanging off you now."

"I should leave more coin this week."

"No maid. What you leave covers more than you eat as it is." She cocked her head to one side appraising Melody, "You look like you did when you first came here. What's wrong?"

Agnes returned balancing plates in a pyramid which Cook indicated this time could go onto the table. Melody waited for Agnes to leave again before she answered.

"I thought if I stayed out of the way, Roman and Abbot would forget about me and I'd forget about them. I've tried these past weeks. I like them both, but I'd be no good as a wife."

Cook frowned, "What makes you think either of them wants you as a wife? Ideas above your station, my girl."

"They ..." Melody dropped her gaze as her cheeks flushed.

"Oh no, don't tell me they've been taking advantage!" Cook was winding herself up to explode again and Melody had to find her voice quickly.

"No! No, nothing like that, I swear! No, Roman gave me a gift, but that's gone now, and Abbot wanted to be around me all the time and I liked talking to him but those people he's with are his kind of people, not me."

Cook waved her hand in the direction of the servant's dining room. "Go and eat your supper."

Once Melody had gone, Cook muttered to herself as she began to fill the large black kettle with water, "His kind of people, indeed. Mister Abbot wants a good shaking."

"Why do I need shaking?"

With her back to the door, Cook hadn't seen Abbot come into the kitchen. She almost dropped the kettle as she spun around.

"Good Lord above, sneaking around like that, you'll put me in my grave!"

Abbot chuckled. "I'm sorry, but you were saying something about me needing a shake?"

Cook took a deep breath to calm her nerves and fixed Abbot with her clear blue eyes.

"Those friends of yours. If that's the kind of life you want, you won't find it here. But you need to think long and hard whether it really is what you want. And that's all I'm saying."

Cook had been with the Cranshaws since David was a baby. She had watched them all grow and shared in their sorrows. She felt it gave her the gravity to speak to both brothers with less deference than she would have otherwise shown, particularly to their father. With their mother mute and feeble, Cook had become the matriarch without anyone objecting.

Abbot felt as if he were six years old and had been caught taking berries from the cold shelf.

"Has Agnes told you they are all leaving tomorrow morning?"

"She has. And all the extra food we got in today will upset Mister Roman no doubt."

"Everything upsets my brother at the moment. Perhaps I should think about making my own way in the world. But..."

Cook waved away his hesitancy. "You can't have your cake and eat it to, you know that. Leave things much longer and you'll miss the boat."

Abbot looked up sharply. "What do you mean?"

"Only that things have a way of sorting themselves out if you don't take the lead. And not always the way you'd want them to. Now, what did you come in here for?"

"Tea," Abbot said quietly, his mind trying to make sense of what Cook was telling him. Could Melody be planning to leave again? Had the comments of Isobel and Eliza upset her that much?

"Go on back to your friends, I'll bring a tray though shortly."

Melody dried the last of the plates at just after eleven o'clock that evening. Cook had gone to her room, leaving instructions for what she wanted left out on the table for the morning. Agnes had also gone up to her small bedroom next to Catherine Cranshaw's. It had been the nursery once, with a connecting door, but with Catherine's declining health it had been decided that Agnes should be installed there so as to be on call if needed in the night.

The gramophone had been switched off, and now only occasional laughter or groans came to Melody's ears through the open windows as game after game of Bridge came to an end. She dried her hands on a towel and picked up the last bucket for the compost heap.

Out in the moonlight she felt the cool breeze, welcome about her neck after the hot kitchen. She had no fear of the night, the sounds were as comforting as the bleating of lambs on a spring morning or the babble of a spring as it trickled over moss-covered rocks. The hush of the trees and an occasional bark or hoot were old friends. As she returned to the kitchen with the now empty bucket, Melody glanced down through the formal garden. A man was standing at the far end, his back to the house, looking out towards Ribble Top field and the woodland beyond.

She had not heard Roman leave the house. Another ripple of laughter came from the drawing room, the light from inside casting oblongs of gold onto the grass. Melody set down the bucket and walked through the garden to where the man remained like a statue illuminated by the moon. She deliberately trod on the gravel path a little way before reaching him, so that he would know she was approaching. He still did not move.

Melody stopped at his side and looked out in the same direction as Roman.

"It's a fair night. Will be colder from now on," she said quietly.

"It is always cold when one is alone."

Melody didn't know how to respond.

"Are you ever lonely, Melody?"

"No, not really."

"But you spend so much time by yourself. Don't you miss the companionship of friends or family?"

"I miss Granfer. And Cicely. But I'm not lonely. People come and go all the time. It does no good to try and cling on if they want to leave." She was thinking of her own mother, but Roman did not know as much of Melody's background as his brother had learned.

"I sometimes wonder what it's all for. All this. We plough, we sow, we reap; an endless treadmill. And I wonder, what if I just stopped. What then? Would people gather round as they did with Mother? The hands would come each day as they always do. The sheep would still eat the grass. Do you know, Melody, sometimes I think I could just stop and no one would notice. And that makes me want to even more."

Again, Melody did not know what to say. She heard the strain in Roman's voice and felt his melancholy but could do nothing to salve him. They stood for some time, gazing out across the top of the trees that loomed as a dark stain on a dip in the horizon. The bell at Robey church proclaimed the half hour. Melody shivered. She turned back towards the house and saw that the drawing room lights had been extinguished.

"They've all gone to bed. It will be quiet enough to sleep now."

"It's not noise that keeps me awake."

"Will you come in?"

"Soon."

Melody wanted to take his arm and lead him back to the farmhouse, yet she dare not. It would be an invitation to intimacy and one she knew she could not retreat from once that step had been taken. Roman was using all of his willpower not to reach out to her, to cling as she had said, as he had in the yard before. The tension was beginning to cause him to shake. If she stayed any longer by his side, he would not be able to stop himself.

As singly as she had come, Melody walked back to the kitchen door, took the bucket inside, and made her way through to the front of the house where she crossed the yard and climbed the ladder to her stable loft.

"You're what?" Roman looked up at his brother.

"I've decided. I shall take a cottage somewhere. Mother can live with me, so you no longer have to deal with her." Abbot had not been able to get Cook's words out of his mind. He needed to take control of his life, and he knew his future lay beyond the farm. After his friends had waved their goodbyes three mornings before, he had been piecing together his plans.

"Don't be absurd. You can't just leave. And Mother will be much better if she stays in surroundings she knows."

"It's no more absurd than hanging around here like a spare part! It's all very well growing a few marrows and tomatoes, but it's not enough! Don't you see, I need to get out. I'm taking the car into Derring this morning to make some enquiries."

Roman stood up from the desk. As usual it was strewn with papers, one or two of which floated down to the floor as he dislodged them.

"Do you understand what you're saying? There will be no income for you if you leave here."

"I have thought it all through. Mother has her income, and I won't be giving up my claim here. You can't have it all, you know!"

"If you're not working here, then you can't expect to keep drawing on the farm. And now I understand why you want to take Mother with you!"

"That's not it at all! I shall go back to law, and Melody will be with Mother. Everything will be perfectly all right, and you can keep making all the decisions here as you have been since we came back."

"Melody? What's she got to do with it?" Roman moved around the desk. More papers fluttered and shifted in their piles.

"She'll be coming with me, naturally. I'll need to find the right sort of place of course, but I'm sure I can convince her that somewhere small will be suitable."

"You can't take her! She's not some ... some piece of furniture!"

"I don't know why you're so against this, Roman. I thought being out of your hair would be the best thing for all of us. It won't be immediately of course, the banns will take three weeks at least, but that will give me time to get everything else organised."

"Banns? You've asked her to marry you?" There was panic now as well as anger in Roman's voice.

"Not yet, no, but I shall. I'm sure she will agree, and she gets along famously with Mother. You'll still have Agnes, of course, and Cook."

"Are you out of your mind? If anyone is going to marry Melody, it will be me. I'm the eldest, it's my right!"

They were standing toe to toe now. This time Abbot was in no mood to back down and walk away.

"You have no right to Melody - she would never agree to marry you!"

"I won't have you disrupt Mother on a whim!"

"What do you care? When was the last time you sat with her?"

"When did you last do a full day's work? Every hour I spend in here is to keep this place going, filling in form after form, quota after quota, just so you can eat and swan about with your friends!"

"Oh, I might have guessed. Jealous because I have friends, and you have no one. Well too bad for you - and I won't let you keep Melody here just to pretend that you have a happy life!"

Roman swung a punch at his brother, which missed, but allowed Abbot to grapple Roman to the floor with a crash. There were no holds barred, both brothers kicking and punching ferociously at each other. Agnes rushed in, gasped at the scene unnoticed by the men, and ran out again to fetch Cook. Moments later Cook appeared with a large basin of cold water which she threw at the writhing pair on the floor. It had the desired effect: both men let go and spluttered to their feet.

"You boys should be ashamed of yourselves! Ashamed! No, I don't want to hear it, take yourselves up to your rooms and change those wet clothes. It's a good thing your father isn't here to see you behaving like wild cats. Atrocious behaviour, the pair of you!" She stood, hands on hips, the basin dripping at her side, waiting for the brothers to do as they were told. Agnes hovered just behind Cook, her hand still over her mouth in shock. Abbot was the first to leave silently. When he had gone, Roman wiped his face with his handkerchief.

"I should fire you for that."

"You'll do no such thing! If you behave like schoolboys then you'll be treated like them, Roman Cranshaw. Don't think I can't guess what it was all about. You two need to sort out who gets what, without beating seven bales out of each other." She turned and shooed Agnes out of the study, leaving Roman stunned that Cook had guessed the reason for the argument.

He took off his pullover and draped it over the back of a chair. Abbot had received most of the water and Roman's shirt was more damp than wet. He decided not to change. He sat down heavily behind the desk once more, elbows on the walnut surface and held his head in his hands. Everything was slipping away from him and he was so very tired of fighting for it all.

Abbot threw his wet shirt onto the floor of his bedroom and tugged his vest over his head. Roman's reaction was outrageous! How dare he assume that he had any rights over Melody, as if she were some thoroughbred horse or prize ram! The hangers in the wardrobe clanged together as Abbot pulled out a fresh shirt; he was too hot for a vest now and would do without. Agitated as he was, he made a hash of buttoning the shirt and had to undo and begin again. The process helped calm him, the adrenalin slowly dissipating.

Legally, Abbot knew that Roman was correct. If he was not working on the farm, he had no claim to an income from it. Only if Roman decided to sell up might some of the profit come Abbot's way. As the youngest son, Abbot had never expected to inherit anything; it had been one of the reasons behind his aspiration to become a lawyer. So now he would focus on building a life away from the farm, and not let it drag him down as it was so clearly doing to Roman.

Abbot combed his wet hair, restoring the side parting. He would need Melody, not only to help look after his Mother, but by his side with her practical abilities which would surely be of use making a cottage into a comfortable home for them all. To convince her, he would need to find just the right cottage – nothing too big and imposing for her. There was no time to lose. He grabbed his jacket and went out.

Melody heard the car roar out of the yard. She had stayed in the stable loft that morning after sleeping beyond sunrise. She had some mending to do, and wanted to test the spinning whorl she had fashioned before making any more. The previous day she had walked along the hedges of the sheep fields and gathered as many tufts of fleece as she could find into a small hessian sack. She had nothing to comb the fleece with, and hadn't washed it, but had picked out most of the vegetation and was about to start teasing a thin twist of fibres when the motor car's engine caught on the crank.

A few moments later, Agnes' face appeared at the top of the ladder.

"You missed a prize fight just now! Both Misters going at it hammer and tongs in the study, and Cook throwing water on them to get them to stop!"

"Are they hurt? Has someone gone to fetch the doctor?"

"No, just their pride I should think. That was Mister Abbot driving off. Cook told me to bring you these." Agnes had carried four large apples in her apron up the ladder. She placed them on the floorboards and perched herself at the top of the steps.

"I was just going to leave them for you; didn't realise you'd be here."

"I've been making a whorl, I thought Jessop might take a few but I'm not sure the notch is deep enough. You'll spin."

"No. I can knit if someone starts me off. Show me how it works."

"You start the thread around here." Melody pointed to the portion of the stick below the wooden disc, "Then the thread comes up and you wrap it so it catches on the notch. Then you spin it and let it hang down while you feed out the fleece so it twists. You do a bit, then wrap it round under the disc, then do a bit more."

Agnes turned up her nose. "Knitting's hard enough without all that rigmarole before you even get started! I'll stick to buying my penny balls of wool."

"I just thought it could be something else to sell. The whorls, not the yarn. I'll make myself some mittens with what I can spin."

"Don't tell me you've made yourself some knitting needles as well!"

"Yes. Cicely has mine."

Agnes shook her head with a smile. "You're a right little Girl Guide! Always prepared or whatever it is they say. I'd better get back. Shall I bring you something over at lunchtime? We could sit in the sun and eat together for a change."

"If you like. You never said what they were fighting about."

Agnes had started to descend the ladder. "Oh, probably the same as usual. Who works hardest on the farm, who doesn't.

Cook said something odd though, she said Mister Roman needs to shoot his arrows if he doesn't want Mister Abbot to run off with the butt. Don't ask me what she means, she's always talking in riddles like that about people. See you at one."

THE FIRST PROPOSAL

By the end of that morning, Abbot was feeling thoroughly ashamed at his naivety when it came to renting a home. He had gone to Derring, having understood Melody's reluctance to move closer to the large town of Audling. He had hoped that a visit to a land agent would result in two or three properties that he could view that afternoon. What he hadn't bargained for was the need to not only pay a considerable portion up front in rent, but also pay the land agent an arrangement fee.

Then had come the embarrassment of having to explain that he was not looking for a large family home, which seemed to be the only properties on offer from several of the land agents. A house the size of the Cranshaw's farm would be far too big for their needs, and Melody would never agree to sleep in one, he knew. There were town houses available, apartments above shops, and several country estates, but very little of the size and price range that Abbot could manage.

He took lunch in the Wyvern Hotel, by that time accepting that everything cost far more than he had realised. Abbot had some savings, mostly from his share of the farm income and one or two small legacies from elderly relations. His war service had been so short, he had not qualified for any pension, and had been demobbed with a few shillings and a service medal along with his discharge papers.

After his lunch, a modest steak and mashed potatoes with a half pint of bitter, Abbot walked back along Derring High Street to the offices of a firm of solicitors that he had spotted earlier. The brass plate by the entrance door proclaimed Messers Kent, Florin and Marshall, Solicitors and Conveyancers, could be found on the first floor of the building and Abbot went up the dark, narrow staircase with as much optimism as he could muster. After almost an hour waiting for one of the partners to become available, Abbot was shown into a large room lined with more books than he had ever seen (and doubted were ever read), and a large, balding man sat behind a large, meticulously tidy desk.

Mr Florin asked Abbot a lot of questions that afternoon, several of which Abbot could not answer. In turn, Abbot asked some questions of his own, and was encouraged that not all of the answers from Mr Florin were negative. At the end of the interview, they shook hands, and Abbot thanked Mr Florin for his time.

"I will, of course, need to discuss the possibility with the other partners." Mr Florin sat back down again after releasing Abbot's hand.

"Of course. You have my address. I look forward to hearing from you if there is anything you can offer me."

It was with significantly more optimism that Abbot then made his way to the next land agent's office. He felt things had turned in his favour, when he was presented with the papers of a small house, to his surprise, located in Robey. The agent was apologetically explaining that it was some way out of Derring, when Abbot stopped him.

"It's quite alright you know; I live not far from Robey as it happens."

"Ahh, then sir will appreciate the peaceful outlook across the headland towards the Channel which can be seen from the bedroom windows. Is sir bringing his family to the village?"

Abbot frowned, "Does that matter?"

"No, sir, not all all, one simply wondered if something larger might be suitable..."

"I think this is a suitable sized property. It is currently empty?"

"Yes, since the end of last month. Fully furnished. A retained gardener, who is custodian of the keys at present. And a very reasonable price."

Abbot arranged to visit the property on his way home that afternoon, having been assured that the gardener would be at home to assist with opening the house. His final task in Derring was the one which made him the most nervous. So much so that he did not go inside the jeweller's shop, but stood for several minutes studying the display of rings in the window. Melody would not want anything ostentatious, he knew, but he could not propose without a ring of some kind. Then he gave himself a hard look in the glass of the jeweller's window: one thing at a time, go and view the house in Robey first.

Roman watched the girls eating their lunch on a bench outside the stable, from the darkness of his study. He glanced at his watch and decided to wait another five minutes before sending Agnes back to her duties. Good staff were difficult to find in such a rural location and Roman had no desire to add the search for a new maid to his growing list of responsibilities. He assumed that day would come eventually; he was aware of Agnes' growing relationship with the young butcher in Robey. Agnes was reliable and competent, and under Cook's eye was worth keeping hold of. If that meant allowing her to have forty minutes for her lunch instead of thirty occasionally, it was a price Roman was willing to pay.

He did not have to separate the girls. Agnes got to her feet as he watched, threw her apple core across the yard for the chickens to squabble over and marched back into the house. Roman listened for the door to close; Agnes' footsteps echoed along the passage way to the kitchen. She would continue straight through the house and out to the strip of grass that bordered the kitchen garden and held the long washing line with its pair of wooden props. The sheets had been billowing in the morning sunshine and needed to be exchanged with a fresh basket once the second batch had been run through the mangle.

Melody remained on the bench after Agnes had gone inside. She turned her face up to the sun and closed her eyes. The summer would not last forever; Avens had told her to always make the most of good weather. The woodlanders of Emmett often developed bowed legs from spending too little time in the sunlight. Melody did not hear the farmhouse door open, but detected the crunch of stones on the cobbled yard and opened her eyes.

"Melody, I need to speak with you."

Anyone else would have got to their feet, but not Melody. She simply sat, expecting Roman to take the space Agnes had recently given up. After a moment, he did so, stretching out his legs and lifting his own face to the sun for a moment.

"You're not working today?"

"On smaller things. Unless you need more hurdles."

"No, the ones you made are sufficient. And well-made," he added. Now that Roman was sitting next to Melody, the words he had been so confident of speaking began to tumble away. He had never felt with anyone else the calmness that he experienced when he was with her. It was almost as if nothing else mattered beyond each moment. But it had to, he reminded himself.

"Melody, I have given your situation some thought. It's all very well for you to sleep in the stable loft while the weather is fine, but come the winter months it really won't be suitable." Roman paused, anticipating either an agreement or a vehement objection.

Melody remained silent.

"With that in mind, I have ... a proposal. You will no longer need to scratch a living making your baskets and laying hedges. It's not a sophisticated life I can offer you here, but with your thoughts on what we could do with the woodland and your ... practical nature, I really feel we will be able to run this place well together. Perhaps even have something to pass on with pride in years to come."

Melody looked at him, frowning. "I don't understand. I have to work. Everyone does."

Roman realised he had not made the full extent of his proposal clear. "Dear girl, I am asking you to be my wife." He gently took hold of her hand.

Melody looked down at her hand in Roman's. It was not an unpleasant sensation.

"I can't think what not working would be like."

"You can still make your things, but you would also have the kitchen garden to supervise, and the rest of the gardens here. I should advise you to leave Cook to manage the kitchen, I don't think she would take kindly to anyone trying to give her orders in her domain," he chuckled.

"What about Abbot?"

"What about him? As I understand it, he plans to seek his fortune elsewhere." There was a touch of bitterness in his response that Roman could not hide, and Melody heard it. She did not, however, understand its meaning. If Abbot was going to leave the farm, did she want to stay there? Roman was talking again.

"I suppose it's a bit of a shock. You'll need to think about it all, no doubt. But that's all right, and I expect you'll want to get used to the idea of living in the house. Naturally if you would prefer your own room, we can arrange that."

Melody slowly withdrew her hand.

"In the house. It's so big. So heavy."

"You don't seem to have any difficulty with it when you come in and read to Mother."

"I can breathe if I sit by a window. But to sleep…"

"Then we shall have your bed beneath a window. I'll leave you to consider it all, but I see no reason to draw things out with a long engagement. We have no one else to please but ourselves."

Roman stood up, smiling again. He felt as if a great weight had been lifted from him, even though Melody had not said yes straight away as he had hoped she might. His offer was on the table, and he did not think Melody would refuse once she weighed up the alternative. He began to whistle a tune as he crossed the yard back to the farmhouse. It was a tune he had heard in the army, many years ago. It had been a long time since he had felt like whistling.

Melody watched him enter the house and close the door again behind him. Marriage. To Roman Cranshaw. Melody didn't think she felt old enough to marry anyone, not least a man who was almost twice her age. It would not be unusual for an eighteen-year-old to marry, although many who did, accepted the ring to legitimise a union previously consummated. Melody did not have that reason to hand.

It would be very cold in the stable loft during the winter nights, Melody had already understood that. With no fire and no stove, even layers of blankets would not keep out the freezing drafts. She did not dread entering the farmhouse now as she had at first, but it still felt oppressive to her. As she had described to Abbot, it felt heavy around her, even when she sat by a window, the sense that the walls and roof were pressing in and down on her was still strong.

Abbot. Of the two brothers he was the one she liked more, though she did not dislike Roman. They were so different to each other; both had good qualities. If only they could have been combined into one person. Had their older brother, David, been the best of them both in one body? Could that be why Catherine Cranshaw had felt the loss of him to be so devastating? Melody wondered what Catherine's husband had been like. There were no photographs in the drawing room or Catherine's bedroom to suggest a man of strength, moral or physical, or one of sinewy activity.

And what of her own family? Vernon and Avens had raised her to be industrious and practical. To be honest, but to recognise that all were equal and no one was better or worse than anyone else simply because of how they chose to live or what they owned. Vernon had been known to turn down work if he felt the employer was dishonourable or treated his other employees poorly. Avens had helped anyone who came to their cabin in whatever way she could. It occurred to Melody that her mother must have been a disappointment to her grandparents.

Betony Trow had never been spoken ill of by Vernon and Avens. They had been silent about her wayward behaviour and answered any questions Melody had in simple and straight forward terms. She could be alive, prosperous, living in a large house with any number of children and a rich husband … Melody felt that this was not the most likely situation for her to find her mother in. It was more probable that she was with some band of performers or show-people, constantly on the move and caring very little for anything other than her next meal or a warm place to sleep.

That brought Melody back to her own immediate needs. She told herself, it really didn't matter what her mother might be doing, or how Vernon and Avens might feel about things now. She had to take care of herself.

Abbot shook the old gardener's hand and walked back to the motor car. The house, for it was more than a small farm worker's cottage, would be perfect for himself, his mother, and of course, Melody. It stood in its own garden, with lime-washed walls and a thatched roof. A picture of centuries past; hollyhocks and scented roses by the door, a large kitchen and newly-installed bathroom, small but bright rooms and the land agent had been correct that from the bedrooms at the front, the sea could be seen sparkling in the distance.

He got into the motor car after cranking the handle a few times and listened for a moment to the engine grumble to itself. He would need to purchase a small car of his own; Roman would never allow him to have the Cowley. If the position with Kent, Florin and Marshall went his way, he would be able to afford a second-hand model, as well as the rent on the house. It felt good to be taking control of his future, rather than simply floating along aimlessly as he had been for so long. It was time to be a man and take on some responsibility. It was time to take a wife.

Melody was in the drawing room with Catherine late that afternoon when Agnes came in to take Catherine to her dinner. Roman had gone out to oversee the replacement of some old stone gate-posts in one of their eastern fields, and the farmhouse was quiet and calm. The two young women gently manoeuvred Catherine out of her chair, Agnes wrinkling her nose at the evidence of the older woman's incontinence.

"We'll need to get you cleaned up and changed before you have your dinner." Agnes looked over Catherine's head at Melody. "It's getting worse. Almost every day now. You'd think she was eighty, not sixty."

"Do you take her to the closet after her lunch?"

"Of course, but I can't wait for her too long. I have to clear the table before the Misters come in for their lunch, when they're here."

"I should take her when I come in. It might help."

"They should get a maid just for her. It's not right to just expect you and me to do more and more. They don't even pay you!"

"I don't mind, really." Melody let go of Catherine's arm so that Agnes could get her through the toilet door.

"You might not, but I do," Agnes said over her shoulder, then nudged the door closed with her hip.

Melody waited outside. It occurred to her that having someone to look after his mother might be a reason for Roman's proposal. She didn't mind spending a couple of hours a day with Catherine, but would she be able to cope with the responsibilities of caring for her all day and night?

Cook was cutting up a pork chop on a plate when the three women entered the dining room, with Catherine in a clean outfit.

"I don't know why I'm doing this, it's your job not mine," she grumbled at Agnes, who rolled her eyes at Melody.

"Leave it then, I'm here now."

"And when are you having yours?" Cook looked directly at Melody.

"I could have it now, and stay with Mrs Cranshaw. If it's ready."

Cook sniffed. "It'll save me putting it on a hot plate. Come and get it."

Melody knew that Catherine did not eat unless the cutlery was put into her hands. She would simply sit and stare at the food; holding the knife or fork seemed to be the trigger she needed to remember how to eat. Once Agnes had started Catherine off, she left Melody to it. Melody was happy to eat in silence. She heard the motor car pull up into the courtyard and the front door open and close. Moments later, Abbot breezed into the dining room, knowing he would find his mother there at that time of day.

His surprise at finding Melody there instead of Agnes only broadened his grin.

"Ahh, both of you together! That will save me having to say everything twice. Is my brother at home?"

"I don't think so."

"Pity, but he made his feelings quite clear on the matter, so I doubt it will make any difference when he hears."

Abbot sat next to his mother, who had finished the small amount on her plate and was looking, as usual, out of the window at nothing in particular.

"Mother, how would you like to live in a very pretty cottage with a view of the sea? You can have your own bedroom, and a cosy sitting room, and the garden has all of your favourite flowers. How does that sound?"

He knew she would not answer, though he had hoped it might provoke some reaction in her. He waited, but Catherine showed no sign of having heard him. Abbot sighed, then looked across at Melody.

"So, it's true; you're leaving," she said flatly.

"It is a perfect cottage, exactly the right size for us, and the gardener has agreed to stay on and look after the vegetable plot. I shan't have much time if I'm successful in gaining the legal secretary's appointment."

"You'll be working as well."

"I hope to, yes. We'll need more than Mother's income to live on, but I think we'll manage." Abbot was still smiling.

"Where is the cottage?"

"That's the best thing: it's at the other end of Robey near the Derring road. Roman will be able to visit Mother whenever he chooses, and I'm sure Agnes and even Cook can make the trip down to see her. I say, if you've had your dinner, why don't we take a walk down now and look at it? Only from the outside, of course, I don't want to trouble the old boy twice in one day, but it would give you an idea of it, at least."

Melody did not want to dampen Abbot's spirits, seeing him so animated and happy about the cottage made her smile along with him. And if he would be staying relatively nearby, then she would still be able to see him occasionally, and Catherine Cranshaw.

"All right. I'll take these plates to the kitchen and let Agnes know your mother has finished."

THE SECOND PROPOSAL

IT WAS A COOL evening. Hazy high clouds had hidden the sun and the air had a hint of autumn in it. Melody had wrapped her shawl around her shoulders, crossed it over her chest and tucked the ends into the back of her belt. Her hair was down as she was not working. She carried one of her own small baskets to harvest more of the swollen blackberries along the way, conscious that the weather could not hold forever and rain would spoil them. Abbot's excitement was such that she realised she would have to collect the blackberries on their way back; he was so keen for her to see the cottage he had found.

Abbot strode out down the lane with Melody matching him easily for speed. She asked him about the position at the solicitors' office, and he explained the tasks he would undertake and how it would eventually lead him to the solicitor examinations.

"You'll miss the farm."

"I don't think so. It's really Roman who makes all the decisions, no matter how much he likes to think we share."

I should tell him of Roman's proposal, Melody thought to herself. Then, seeing Abbot smile, she knew it would upset him to think that Roman had a claim on her. She had not agreed to Roman's offer; she was still her own woman, and she would not spoil Abbot's evening.

They walked past the church of Saint Michael, the old forge and the Bellows Inn. Around the corner of the main street, Jessop was bringing in his wares from the roadway outside his shop window. He tapped the side of his head to acknowledge Abbot, and nodded at Melody, but said nothing as the pair passed by. They continued past the small butcher's shop where Agnes' beau, John Stoneham worked, and then had Melody known, they also passed Mrs Pennard's cottage. Her front garden was a shadow of its spring glory, with many of the plants now showing bronzed and brittle leaves. A clump of Michaelmas daisies grew by Mrs Pennard's low garden wall. Abbot plucked one and offered it to Melody.

"They grow all around the village, always have, like weeds."

"There are purple ones in Emmett, much taller than these white ones."

"People here wear them on their lapels and the women braid them around their bonnets for the Michaelmas Fair. I wonder if being closer to a community, one that has activities such as fairs and such like, might do Mother some good."

"What do they do for the fair here? Do they have feasting? Is there a fire?" Melody suddenly ached for the Candlemas celebrations of her childhood.

"It starts with the harvest festival at Saint Michael's. The village school children deliver the produce to the elderly, and then there are the usual events during the week. A whist drive, a recital, a few games of Ropes on the grass behind The Bellows, a tea dance in the village hall on the Saturday afternoon. Would you like to go to the dance?"

Melody bit her lip. "I don't know any dances."

"I'm sure you'll pick the steps up easily, it's really only walking around in a big circle. Ahh, here we are!"

Abbot stopped at the garden gate of the cottage, opened it and indicated that Melody should pass through. Melody was relieved that the question of dancing could be ignored at least for now. She looked up at the thatched roof, recognising the pattern along the ridge and the swan crafted out of straw which was secured in the centre of the apex of the roof.

"That's Tamp's thatch."

Abbot followed her gaze. "Do you mean the style of it?"

"No, I meant Tamp thatched it. That's his mark, the swan. There was another we passed just before Jessop's, was one of his too." She turned around and pointed back towards the village centre. "See the one with the wheel? That's the Kennet's mark."

"I see. I'd not noticed it before, but now you've pointed it out, yes, I see the wheel. Does every thatcher have their own mark like that?"

"All I've known do. Granfer would cut reeds for Puck and Tom Redrow some years, across the Wynn. They had a fish as their mark."

"Do you know, I have lived here in Wynn Vale my whole life, twenty-six years, and there is so little I know about it all. You teach me something new every time we are together." They were standing very close to each other, the dying light picking out the sun-bleached strands of Melody's lose hair.

Melody turned back to the house and walked up to the sitting room window. She cupped her hands around her face to look inside. The room she saw was furnished with a pair of fireside chairs and a low double seat with cushions and a blanket thrown across it. An old rug lay in front of the fireplace between the chairs. Small paintings hung on the walls in simple frames, and a dark wood cupboard ran the length of the wall opposite.

"The windows allow a good amount of light all day I should think," Abbot said, hopefully. "Shall we look around the back?"

Melody followed him, pushing a large fuchsia out of their way to get to the back garden. There was a small rectangle of lawn which gave onto deep flower beds. The gardener clearly took pride in his work and the lawn edges were clipped with precision. Beyond the borders, there was a strip of untended land, then a fence with pasture that rose gently to a small copse on the horizon. Melody recognised the outline of the tall straight ash trees. As she was looking out across the field, Abbot tried the kitchen door and found it open.

"I say, what a stroke of luck! Come on, you can see inside as well."

"We shouldn't." Melody turned reluctantly away from the trees.

"Why not? I had permission this afternoon, I'm sure it extends for as long as the place is open."

He went inside and Melody followed with some hesitancy. It was a pretty cottage, and had been thoughtfully extended over the years to almost double its original size. Abbot encouraged Melody to view the bedrooms on her own. He wanted her to fall in love with the view of the sea without him prompting her. He waited nervously in the dining room with its window looking out at the side of the cottage over the vegetable plot.

Melody touched the uneven stone of the white-washed walls with her fingertips in the hallway before climbing the wooden staircase. It was cool inside the cottage and she was glad of her shawl. The first bedroom she looked into without entering. It was at the rear of the cottage, and she could see directly through the window from the doorway to the ash trees on the ridge.

The front bedrooms were larger; one gave a view of the field opposite with a large oak tree standing almost in its centre. From that angle, the oak blocked most of the rest of the landscape although in winter it would be possible to see the headland beyond. The largest bedroom was not in a direct line with the oak, and had the view that Abbot had been enthralled by. With the oak to the left, from that window the slope of the headland met the horizon and a stretch of water filled the gap before the land rose again on the right. A tiny portion of the Derring road was visible as it climbed the right-hand plane.

Though Melody had considered running away to sea, it held no real interest for her. She crossed the landing again and went into the smaller room at the back. It had no furniture, unlike the other rooms, and had not been used for some time. Its ceiling was plain wooden boards, unpainted. It reminded her of the cabins of Emmett Wood. The window was laced with cobwebs, but Melody worked the catch loose and opened one side. If only there was a view from the farmhouse like this, she mused. If only the farmhouse didn't feel so dark and heavy every time she went into it.

Just as Abbot was considering calling out to Melody to make sure she was alright, he heard her footsteps on the stairs.

"What do you think? Did you see the sea?"

"I did. I think your mother will like it here."

"Excellent! We will keep the gardener on, as I said, and I'm sure there will be some young girl in the village who can come in and do for us."

"We should get back. The sun is almost down."

Melody went through the kitchen, picking up her basket from where she's left it by the door, and out into the garden. She realised she had not taken a deep breath as she usually did each time she left the farmhouse. Perhaps she should look for a position as a companion to an elderly lady in a house like the cottage, as Agnes had been telling her about. Agnes said she had seen two or three advertisements in the newspaper recently for such vacancies, and had pointed out that it was practically what Melody had been doing with Catherine Cranshaw. It would be like sitting with Cicely's Great-Grammer and listening to her stories, Melody thought.

They began the walk back up to the farm, Melody carrying her basket between her and Abbot.

"I shall go back to the agent on Monday and tell him we'll take it from the beginning of next month. I'll need to line up some employment if the legal secretary job doesn't come through, but I'm sure I can find something. Then of course we'll need to arrange the wedding, and move some of Mother's things down from the farm. We won't be rich by any means, but I think we can live comfortably..."

Melody stopped abruptly in the middle of the lane.

"What wedding?" Had Roman told Abbot before asking her? Was Abbot moving out because Roman wanted her to move in?

Saint Michael's church bell began to strike seven o'clock.

"Blast! I was going to wait until I'd bought a ring, but I've rather let my mouth run away with things." Abbot looked sheepishly at Melody. "Our wedding, Melody. I want to marry you. If you'll have me?"

The last of the sun was in his eyes and he couldn't see the colour drain from Melody's face.

"Abbot, I ..." Melody wanted to tell him about Roman's proposal. She wanted to tell him that the thought of living in the farmhouse left her cold inside, and that the sight of the ash stand from the cottage window each morning might be enough to overcome her distrust of solid buildings. The words would not come.

The silence between them stretched until Abbot raised his hand to shield his eyes and the last chime of the hour sounded.

"I should have waited. I'm really no good at all of this. You must have a ring, of course."

Melody took a slow step towards him. She swallowed, trying to organise the words before speaking them.

"I am not long eighteen. Everything has changed this year; things go wrong for me. I don't think I am good luck."

"Melody, nothing that has happened has been your fault."

Melody shook her head. "I don't want to bring you bad fortune."

They began walking again, slowly towards Saint Michaels where the lane forked off to the farm.

Abbot was frowning. He felt his plans slipping away from him but was aware that if he pushed Melody for an answer, her first response would be to run away. He understood now that was how she coped: he was frightened that the next time she might run too far for him to find her again. An idea came to him.

"How do your people arrange their unions? Is there a particular church that you all use?"

"Some go to Emmett Green. The men who work at the sawmills have to be married right to get their extra shilling. Not everyone though. The elders have to agree."

"Do you need to ask their permission."

Melody considered the question for a moment. If she still lived in Emmett, she would have asked her Granfer if there had been someone she had wanted to start a cabin with.

"I don't know who they would have chosen as elder now."

Abbot realised Melody was referring to Vernon and changed tack.

"What else happens? Is there some great feasting that happens?"

"Sometimes. Mostly the families get together and decide which grove the cabin or van will be in. They'll eat together if they're on good terms. Most are. Both families build the cabin, or if it's to be a van, then the men will fetch it in with the horses. The women help with cooking things and bedding. We call it cabin dressing." Melody made a sound that resembled a gulp or a hiccough. In talking about it, she had realised once again that she no longer had the support of the woodlanders around her.

"It all sounds very civilised ... I mean, without a great deal of fuss. If you wanted a big show, then of course we could, but I think I would prefer something small and private."

Melody didn't reply. She was still thinking of the new cabins she'd helped fill with embroidered linen and blankets over the years. Avens had always been working on some piece of sewing in the evenings when it was too warm to knit. Melody wondered if Cicely had started her cabin dressing yet. Mendy Barrowford had been spending more time at the Hurst's cabin over the previous winter, and Melody knew Cicely liked him.

Abbot decided not to push any further. The proposal had been made, and now he would have to wait for Melody to decide. He would take the cottage either way, although he would need to find someone to sit with Catherine Cranshaw once he started his employment.

When they reached the edge of the woodland on the Cranshaw's property, Melody told Abbot to carry on without her.

"I know it's getting dark, but I wanted to pick some berries for Cook. I won't stay long."

Abbot looked up and down the lane as if to make sure there were no dangers waiting to spring out at Melody the moment his back was turned. Satisfied that she would be safe, he nodded his head. Melody disappeared through the undergrowth.

As they had been approaching the trees, Melody had begun to hope that the rook she had named Archer might be making his regular patrol of the fields beyond the woodland's edge. She hurried through the trees, her feet following the path they had worn over the summer. Archer might already be up in the rookery preparing to settle for the night with his flock. Every so often the birds would rise up in a scattering of wings and agitated 'chaak, chaak' calls before calming down again.

Archer was not in the field as Melody emerged. She scanned the pasture but her only company were a handful of rabbits. Deflated, Melody turned back to the banks of brambles that cascaded out of the undergrowth and began to pick blackberries for her basket. They were over-ripe and many squashed between her fingers as she tried to pluck them from the bushes.

How could she choose between the brothers? Roman offered stability, a home, and there was an undeniable attraction between them. But he was so much older than she was. Abbot was closer to her in age, and they had found a more comfortable relationship, but could he really afford the cottage? If his hopes of the legal secretary position fell through, what else could he turn his hand to? Melody did not think he had many practical skills, beyond growing vegetables.

Melody had stopped picking and was sucking the berry juice from her fingers. It was almost dark now, with just a thin line of gold along the crest of the western hills. A sound behind her made Melody turn around. Archer the rook regarded her from six feet away, his head cocked to one side.

"You came! Wait, I have something ..." Melody dug her hand into her apron pocket and pulled out a piece of broken hard biscuit. She had saved it from breakfast in case she had felt hungry later. She broke the biscuit into smaller pieces and threw them to roughly halfway between her and the bird. Archer paced two feet to the right, eyed the crumbs, paced three feet to the left, then gave a half-jump-half-flight towards Melody and began to eat the treats.

Melody sank down onto the grass, ignoring the dew that would make her skirt damp.

"What am I to do, Archer? They both want to marry me and whichever I choose, the other is sure to be cross. I don't want them to be fighting over me again." She watched the rook make its way steadily along the line of biscuit, wondering if it was listening to her at all. More likely just intent on filling its belly before nightfall, she suspected.

"I could run away. Properly this time; go as far as I could before anyone noticed. But I don't want to be completely on my own, and there's Agnes here, and Cook, even though she's fierce. Then there's Mrs Cranshaw; I don't know that I really want to be an old lady's companion like Agnes said I could. I like her well enough, but all I do is a bit of reading. I couldn't do what Agnes does with the washing and dressing. And no doubt Mrs Cranshaw will need that sooner or later."

The rook finished the last biscuit crumb and shook itself. Satisfied that its feathers were in the correct order, it took a tentative step closer to Melody in case she had any more food in reserve. Melody opened her hands to show they were empty. The rook promptly turned its back and launched itself up with a laborious flap of wings. Melody watched it join the rookery which was now a purple outline against a navy-blue sky. A general welcoming chorus sounded, quickly subsiding into the wind.

"At least I understand what you want, old bird. You're easy to please, and you don't much care whether I'm here or not. I wish people were more like you." Melody got to her feet and picked up her basket.

"A sorry offering," she muttered to herself as she began her walk back to the lane. "Why do men have to make things more difficult than they needed to be? We could have all just lived as we started, me in the hut and everyone else in the house, and there'd have been no trouble without Holden Prentice sticking his nose in where it's not wanted. Now it's all got to change again, but why? Why do they both want to marry me?"

There was a faint stirring of the treetops as a breeze came in from the sea. Melody thought she heard the rookery again. She realised she was asking the right question, but of the wrong audience.

MELODY CONSIDERS HER OPTIONS

"Sorry, Cook! Is there any supper left for me?" Abbot had entered through the kitchen, knowing that dinner had long since been cleared away from the dining room by Agnes.

"Plate on the stove for you. Though no doubt the broad beans will be hard as bullets by now."

"You're an angel."

Abbot ate his meal at the kitchen table, glanced out of the kitchen window at the darkness of the garden, then went in search of his brother.

Roman had for once managed to get through a day without telephone calls causing his blood pressure to rise. Having asked Melody to be his wife, he had felt a growing sense of peace, the like he had not experienced in a very long time. The offer was on the table, it was undoubtedly attractive, and he was hopeful of a positive conclusion though he acknowledged there may need to be some further negotiations. After dinner he read to his mother for a while, then as Agnes took Catherine upstairs, Roman poured himself a whisky and sat with his legs stretched out and feet up on the fender of the fireplace. The fire was made up but not lit; it would not be long before the autumn evenings were illuminated by the farm's own seasoned logs blazing there.

Abbot entered the drawing room and took the wide, worn leather chair on the other side of the fireplace. It had been their father's favourite. He noted the glass in his brother's hand, but felt no need to pour himself a drink.

"I have to tell you, brother, I have decided to take a cottage down in Robey."

"So you mean to go through with it."

"I do. From the first of next month. I have made enquiries in Derring and hope to have a position in a solicitors' office secured very soon also."

Roman nodded. It would solve one or two of the negotiations he had been contemplating if Abbot were no longer resident at the farm.

"Are you still insisting that Mother goes with you?"

"I think it would be good for her. To be around people more often. Did you know, they have a weekly afternoon bingo in the church hall? The Women's Institute meet once a month and the Vicar tells me they are always happy to welcome volunteers to arrange the flowers and polish the brasses in the church. It will take time, of course, but I'm sure Melody will encourage her to mix with the locals."

"Melody?" Roman sat up sharply and looked directly at his brother.

"Yes. I have asked her to marry me."

The two men held each other's gaze for a long moment in silence. Then Roman finished his drink in a single gulp.

"Did she tell you that I also have asked her to be my wife?"

"You ... But you knew that I was going to propose to her!"

"Yes, and it made me realise how improved life would be here if she were to become a permanent member of the family. Didn't she tell you that?"

Abbot frowned. "No, she did not. Did she give you an answer?"

"Not yet. Though I do not intend to wait indefinitely. I assume your plans rely on her consent?"

There was a pause before Abbot replied. "I hadn't thought that she would say no. But I suppose... it would take some other arrangements, but no, I intend to take the cottage regardless and with any luck pick up my legal career where I left off." He looked into the fireplace and said, half to himself, "What a predicament we have created for Melody."

"I expect she will make the right choice. She needs stability."

She needs freedom, Abbot thought to himself, and immediately wondered if marriage to anyone would give Melody that. He got to his feet slowly and offered Roman his hand.

"May the best man win."

Roman was surprised at the gesture. He had been sure there would be a repeat of the physical confrontation they had had earlier once Abbot found out about his proposal. He shook Abbot's hand without standing.

"I'm sure he will."

A fine drizzle was falling the next morning as Melody crossed the farmyard. She knew that once Agnes had shuffled Catherine Cranshaw along from the dining room to the drawing room, the older woman would be left alone there, by the window, until lunchtime. Melody took a deep breath as she turned the handle on the front door and let herself in. It was never locked. She would normally walk around the house and enter by the kitchen door, but this day she did not want to have to explain to Cook why she was indoors.

The hallway was dark and cool. Melody could hear the drag of a brush against carpet somewhere near the top of the staircase. Big houses took a lot of looking after, she thought, as she went along the hall to the drawing room. Melody paused outside the slightly open door, listening for voices. She heard none, pushed the door open and went inside.

Catherine turned her head in Melody's direction and a glimmer of recognition showed in the small smile she gave.

"Rosemary," she whispered.

Melody smiled and picked up a stool to sit on next to Catherine's chair.

"Good morning, Mrs Cranshaw. It's early, but I wanted to talk to you about something particular." Melody watched the older woman, hoping for some kind of acknowledgement.

Catherine looked at Melody. It was not a blank look; she was focused on Melody and seemed interested in what she had to say. Melody continued.

"Your sons. Roman and Abbot. They both want to marry me."

Catherine made no response.

"I'm telling you first, because I believe they won't have asked you. They should have." Melody watched the woman's face for any sign of disapproval, but there was none. Catherine's dark blue eyes simply watched Melody as she spoke.

"Roman is the eldest. He will always live here, and he wants me to live here. I don't know that he loves me, but he likes me and I like him."

Catherine smiled very briefly, then it was gone.

"Abbot cares for me, I know that. He wants to live in Robey."

A slight frown crossed Catherine's brow; if Melody had not been paying attention she would have missed it.

"I think Abbot wants the best for me, and for you…" Melody paused, no frown returned, "…but I don't know if that's a reason to get married. And you mustn't worry that there is a reason, because your sons are gentlemen and nothing has happened that shouldn't have." Melody felt her own cheeks heat up as her thoughts lingered over what had not happened.

She waited to see if any further reaction came from Catherine. Melody had not expected a two-way conversation; she simply felt that Catherine should be included in her decision-making. Two of her three options would mean the two women would share a home, and Melody understood that would be different to spending an hour or two together every couple of afternoons.

Catherine heard each word Melody spoke. She recognised the names of her sons. She liked the girl sitting in front of her in the drawing room and who came to read to her some days. The girl reminded her of a friend she once had, Rosemary, who had laughed and danced around all the young men while Catherine only had eyes for Robert Cranshaw. Then Rosemary had gone away and Catherine had not seen or heard from her again. Catherine knew this girl was not Rosemary, but she could not help the name escaping each time she saw Melody, they looked so similar.

Melody decided a straight question might be a better approach.

"If I marry Roman, would you be happy?"

Catherine did not say his name, but her mouth made the shape of Roman's name.

"If I marry Abbot?"

Again, no sound but the shape of her younger son's name on Catherine's lips. Melody breathed out and smiled at Catherine. At least she had not reacted badly, Melody acknowledged. She stood up.

"I'll come back later and read to you. This afternoon, like usual."

Catherine smiled again as Melody patted her shoulder.

Back in the hallway, Melody listened to the sounds of the house. Agnes was still sweeping upstairs. Cook could be heard humming to herself in the kitchen. Melody turned towards the study. The door was closed. Melody had not seen or heard Roman leave the farm that morning; she assumed that he would be in the study working. Abbot had gone with the farm hands that morning to begin ploughing and to bring in the last of the leeks.

Melody knocked on the door.

"Yes!"

She opened the door, still running through the words she had practiced late into the night before.

"Melody! This is unexpected. Have you come to your decision already?" Roman was as usual sitting behind a pile of papers at the desk. His shirt sleeves were rolled up to his elbows and he wore a sleeveless pullover of dark green. "Sit down, won't you."

Melody went to the chair Roman had indicated and sat on the edge of the seat. She made fists with her hands and looked directly at Roman across the desk.

"Why do you want to marry me?"

It was not what Roman had expected to hear. He placed the cap on his pen and sat back in his chair.

"Does it matter?"

"I should like to know."

"Very well. If I were to take any wife, she would have to sympathetic to my plans for the farm. I'll not pretend that you and I would be a love match, but that may come in time and you cannot deny there is a certain attraction between us. I need a wife who will support my ideas, and work with me to see them realised. If children follow, all to the good. I should like to leave this place one day to my offspring, but hopefully that day will be some way off. With my mother in her current condition, we have not kept abreast of local society. I should like to put that right, and to do that you would have free rein to entertain friends, within our financial limits of course." He leaned forward in his chair and rested his hands on the desk. "Does that help with your decision?"

Melody nodded once, not wanting to give any of her thoughts away.

"I know that my brother has also proposed marriage to you." Roman continued, "He cannot provide the security that I can, you must surely see that. He has only a small income, barely enough to support himself."

"Thank you. I'm sorry to have disturbed you." Melody stood up to leave.

"Wait a moment, there is nothing here that cannot wait. Melody, I am sincere in my proposal. I do believe we would make a strong and compatible union. I hope you will not let the age gap weigh too heavily on your decision." His voice had lost the self-assured edge he had adopted when answering her question.

"I need to think some more."

"Of course. Just don't leave it too long. I am keeping no secrets from you; I believe we understand each other."

Melody went back to the stable loft; the rain fell with more determination and puddles had formed in the uneven cobbles of the farmyard. She exchanged pleasantries with one of the stable boys who was mucking out the stalls before climbing the ladder to her own space. Melody picked up the spinning whorl and handful of discarded fleece from her bed and began to spin out more yarn.

Roman had said nothing that she had not already considered. He was correct, theirs was not a love match, and yet… there was an attraction between them, an almost instinctive understanding. Melody was interested in learning more about Roman's plans for the woodland and whatever else he was hoping to do with the farm. However, the idea of having to host parties and entertain other couples from the area, people who would naturally be more like Roman and less like her, left her cold. She would not fit in. They would be like Abbot's friends, with their gay clothes and music. It would be expected of her to make the arrangements, and give instruction to Agnes and Cook. Melody did not think she could do that, and even if she tried, she could imagine the look on Cook's face and the way she would clatter around the kitchen when she felt put out by what the family asked of her even now.

By the time Abbot and the farmhands arrived back at the yard, the rain had wrung itself out and pale grey clouds lay over the distant hills of Wynnfallow. Melody listened to the chatter of the men outside. The stable boy brought the horses inside and rubbed them down and fed them. Melody was about to put down the whorl and take up some of the green willow that she had cut earlier that week, when she heard Abbot's voice in the stable below. He was telling the boy that he could get off for his supper and that Abbot would finish the feeding and watering. Melody decided to take the opportunity to speak with Abbot and descended the ladder.

"Ah! I wondered if you might be here. It's been heavy going with the plough today but we've done as much as we can for now. What have you been up to?" Abbot tipped a bag of oats into a trough, ready to be soaked in water overnight.

"I've been spinning. I want to ask you something."

"Give me two minutes to finish this. Oh, and we're going to be dipping the sheep next week so your hurdles will see some action. I'm sure they will stand up to all the battering they'll get. Right, what did you want to ask?" He put the bucket, now empty of water, on the ground beside the trough and stood up straight. Even in his old working clothes, Abbot cut a fine figure with his blonde hair in need of a trim.

"Why do you want to marry me?"

"Gosh, what a question! Where does one start?" He ran his hand through his hair.

Melody waited.

"I suppose, you've run away from us once, and I don't want you to feel as though you have to again." He took a step towards her. "I've made up my mind to stand on my own feet, away from here, and I can't imagine doing so without you. I don't know if this is love, Melody, but I very much like you. I care about you. We get along well, wouldn't you say?"

Melody leaned against the ladder and folded her arms. "We do."

Abbot laughed, "You are so unlike any girl I've known! Perhaps that's it, perhaps that's why I want to marry you. But look here, I've given it some thought today. It's a good little scheme you've established with your baskets and things for Jessop to sell in his shop. I wouldn't expect you to give it all up, you know. Heaven knows we might need the income if I don't get the secretary position I'm after." A thought occurred to him, "You didn't think I'd asked you, just to be a skivvy or look after Mother, did you?"

"You would need someone for her."

"Yes, but that's not why I asked you. It just all seemed to fit together once I'd started thinking about it. I asked you for purely selfish reasons, but nothing to do with Mother, I assure you."

Melody wasn't sure she completely believed him, but found that she wanted to.

"I know that my brother has also asked you to be his wife. I can't offer you a grand house, Melody, but I don't think that's really what you want in any case. I can offer more than a stable loft though, if you want it. I'd better go and wash up ready for dinner." He turned to leave the stable, but stopped by the door and looked back at Melody. "If you want me."

Had Melody been a regular, or even occasional, patron of the cinema in Derring or Audling, she would have known that that was her cue to sprint across the stable and fall into Abbot's arms. Even Agnes would have recognised it for the invitation it was. However, Melody simply nodded once, turned and began to ascend the ladder once more, leaving Abbot no nearer his goal. He proceeded into the house, perplexed at the situation, yet intrinsically understanding that as he had said, Melody was not like any girl he had ever known.

Back in the stable loft, Melody picked up the bundle of willow from the floor and began to sort through it selecting the whips to use for the base of a new basket. Not for her the wistful gaze out of a window to contemplate the information she had just gleaned. Melody thought while she worked. Abbot had answered the questions she had left unasked. The position of the two brothers was now much clearer to her, and she knew at least what she did not want her future to be. That left only for her to decide what she did want, and what alternatives there might be. For that exercise, Melody needed a newspaper.

Agnes found Melody later that evening at the servant's dining table, with a week old newspaper spread out in front of her. A half-eaten bowl of stew and a thick slice of buttered bread were at her elbow.

"What you looking for?" Agnes put her own bowl on the table and sat opposite Melody.

"What's going on away from here."

Agnes could see the situations vacant columns were holding Melody's attention.

"Not so many jobs as there used to be. Everything's getting more expensive. Johnnie was saying only yesterday that they've had to put their prices up again. I don't know if we'll ever man-age to save enough to get married."

Melody looked up from her reading. "Does it cost a lot?"

"Well, it's not the ceremony itself, though you have to pay for the choir if you want them, and a new frock, and a bit of a party afterwards. But that's just the day. It's the house and the furniture and then the kiddies when they come along, and of course I'd not be working so it would be all down to Johnnie."

None of this had occurred to Melody. In Emmett, the families helped set up a young couple in their caravan or cabin, and both man and wife would continue much as they had before even with small children around them. Then Melody remembered that Agnes was to all intents and purposes an orphan and had been expected to go into service as soon as she was fourteen. There were few orphans in Emmett, and those unfortunate enough to find themselves with such a label were taken in by another family under the direction of the elders.

"So you would stay in Robey when you marry Johnnie."

"Oh yes. Though I'm not moving in with him and his mother! I've told him, we have our own little house, or a long engagement. Ugh! Broad beans again, she knows I can't stand them!" Agnes pulled a face as she swallowed a mouthful of stew, and the proceeded to pick through the contents of her bowl with her spoon to find any more of the offending articles. "You want these?"

Melody pushed her own bowl across the table to receive Agnes' beans.

"What is a 'percolator'?"

"No idea. Read me the advert."

"It says, 'assemblers wanted for production of electrical percolators, manual dexterity a must, women considered, twenty-one shillings a week.' It's in Derring."

"Factory work." Agnes dipped her bread into the stew, "No good for the likes of you. Being cooped up in a factory all day doing the same thing over and over. The pay sounds all right, but you wouldn't last more than a week."

Melody bristled at the assumption.

"I can work hard. You don't know what you can do until you try."

"Yes, but factories are big and noisy and smelly and dirty. Hundreds of people in and out, dangerous too. Especially with those electrical things. Give a body a nasty shock and your hair would stand on end! Anyway, you've got a nice set up here, though why you won't take one of the bedrooms I don't know. What are you looking at positions for?"

"I wanted to see what I might be able to do. Most of it is jobs like yours. Or it says no women."

"You want to find yourself a nice young man with a good job who wants to take care of you, like in the magazine stories. Like my Johnnie. Here, I could see if he has any friends, and we could all go for a picnic one Sunday. That would get you meeting new people."

"Mmm." Melody did not look up from the newspaper. It was not picnic weather, and adding more suitors to her list was not something she wanted to do; things were complicated enough. It was clear to her from the situations vacant that she would find it difficult to secure any employment were she to leave the Cranshaw's farm. Without employment, there would be nowhere safe to sleep. He options appeared to be limited to the two offers before her, and she would have to decide between them.

Agnes Has News

It did not take many more hours for Melody to make her mind up. When she woke the next morning, with the rain drumming on the stable roof, she knew in her heart which of the brothers she would have a chance at happiness with. Now she would have to let one of them down and hope it would not sour things between her and them, or further between the brothers themselves.

Her clothes felt damp as she hurriedly dressed. The stables really were not designed for human occupation, unlike the Emmett cabins with their inner walls keeping a layer of straw sandwiched as insulation against the outer boards. Melody picked up the end of bread and wedge of cheese she had brought back for her breakfast, and realised the waxed paper had a hole in it. Mice! She should have borrowed a tin from Cook. It was inevitable, and Melody chuckled to herself that it had taken the rodents much longer to discover her provisions than she had expected. She broke off the nibbled end of cheese and pulled off pieces of bread until she was satisfied she would not catch anything from any small animal's teeth. If she had her own kitchen, she could be sure to keep it clean and safe from infestation. The idea was growing in attraction.

Melody listened for the voices of the farmhands as they gathered in the yard. She knew they would be there for fifteen or twenty minutes, sheltering under the stable eves until either Roman or Abbot came out with their work details for the day. The smoke from a woodbine cigarette drifted up through the slightly open window in the loft. That would be old Harry Petty. He was always the first there, though he was leaving his home in Robey earlier and earlier now, to arrive at the same time as he always had.

The Roaker twins came next. Slow-witted, they had worked on the farm since they were boys scaring crows in the fields. Melody could never tell Peter from Paul. They would have been a liability on the battlefield and their mother was spared the news that had broken Catherine Cranshaw.

Presently Abbot could be heard greeting the men. Melody listened to his voice, a smile coming to her lips. She could see him in her mind's eye, standing in the yard, getting soaked just like the men, directing them to the fields despite the weather. Then she heard the clank of tools and the squeak of the wheelbarrow wheel. And then the yard was quiet again. Melody tied her boot laces, put her shawl around her shoulders and climbed down the ladder.

Roman Cranshaw was finishing his breakfast in the dining room. He would be taking the motorcar into Audling that morning for an appointment with the bank manager. Agnes was clearing away Catherine's plate and cup, in readiness to lead the lady along to the drawing room for her morning station.

"Agnes, do you think Mother looks a little brighter this morning?" Roman helped himself to more coffee.

"She's eaten both eggs, sir. That's not like her at all." As she spoke, Catherine reached for the toast rack and began to pull at a slice of bread.

Agnes and Roman exchanged a look, then Agnes lifted the toast rack and placed it next to Catherine. The older woman prised a slice from the holder and immediately brought it to her mouth to take a bite.

"Oh ma'am! Wouldn't you like some butter on it first? Here, let me." Agnes gently took the toast and placed it on the remaining plate. She spread a little butter and cut the slice in half. Catherine set about the toast again with vigour.

"Extraordinary!" Roman could not remember the last time his mother had taken food of her own volition.

It was into this domestic scene that Melody walked. She had seen the study door was open and guessed that the family would still be in the dining room.

"You're out and about early," Agnes said over her shoulder as she piled cups and plates onto a large tray. "Missus Cranshaw's got her appetite back today too. Toast as well as eggs!"

"Thank you, Agnes." Roman indicated to a chair, "Sit down, Melody." His tone left Agnes in no doubt that she was no longer required.

They waited until Agnes had left the room.

"Have you come to a decision?"

"I have. I can't marry you. I'm not the right girl for you. What you want isn't me."

Catherine sat chewing her toast slowly.

Roman put down his coffee cup and dabbed his mouth with a napkin.

Agnes returned, leaving the empty tray on the end of the sideboard. "Come along now Missus Cranshaw, you can bring your toast."

She got the woman to her feet and with one of Agnes' hands under her elbow and the other carrying the plate, they made their way out of the dining room.

Melody stood up and made to follow Agnes and Catherine.

"There's no need to dash off, sit down, please."

Reluctantly, Melody retook her seat.

"Coffee?"

Melody shook her head.

Roman sighed. "You say you are not what I want. I assure you, that is not true."

"You want a wife like Abbot's friends. Someone who will host your parties and have an education and be able to talk to you of business and money. That's not me. It's not what I want."

"You could learn. You have a sharp mind, I'm sure you would pick it all up in no time."

"That's what I mean. It's not who I am. You don't want me, Roman. You might want a wife, but not me."

She held his gaze, her lips set firm, hands clenched in her lap. He looked at her, with wisps of hair escaping from her clasp and laying wet on her shoulders. He could love her; he could watch her bloom into a woman with a prosperous estate and enjoy children and his old age with her at his side. But in that moment, he knew she was correct in her assessment of his motives. It made him want her all the more for her astuteness.

"Perhaps you need more time ..." As he said the words, he knew it was futile.

Melody shook her head once more. "No. I've made up my mind."

"And I cannot persuade you otherwise?"

"No. There will be a girl for you somewhere. You are a nice man. But we cannot ..." she did not need to finish the sentence. Melody stood again and this time Roman did not call her back.

Instead of returning to the stable loft, Melody went into the drawing room. The toast had disappeared from the plate and Agnes was nowhere to be seen. Catherine turned her head as she heard Melody enter.

"Rosemary." Catherine spoke louder than Melody had heard before, and a smile was plainly animating her face. It was a face smeared with butter.

Melody went to the older woman, and picked up the napkin from her lap.

"You've butter on your cheek, here." Melody gently wiped the woman's face. She found herself smiling back at Catherine. Melody moved the empty plate to a side table and perched herself on the seat of a nearby chair.

"You heard what I said to Roman in there."

Catherine continued to smile. Did she nod her head? Melody could not be sure.

"I've decided that I will marry Abbot. Does that make you happy?"

"Rosemary." Catherine was still smiling.

Melody patted her hand.

"I'll come and read to you later. I need to finish a basket first. If the rain stops, I need to take them down to Jessop. I'll be back."

Agnes bustled in with a towel over her shoulder and a bowl of warm water.

"Oh! Has she finished the toast? I thought it would be easier to clean her up in here. Everything all right?"

Melody stood up and moved out of Agnes' way. "I think so."

As Melody reached the drawing room door, she heard the word, "Happy." She turned to see Agnes staring in amazement at Catherine Cranshaw, who was in turn looking at Melody.

"Well I never did! That's the first new word she's said in years." Agnes exclaimed.

Melody smiled and went back to her baskets.

She found it difficult to concentrate. The rain continued to patter on the stable roof, and she found she continually mis-counted the willow whips in their pattern. Eventually she put the half-finished basket onto the floor and lay on her back, on her bed of straw.

How would it be, to live in the cottage in Robey with Catherine Cranshaw all day, she wondered. Could she bear to be relied upon so heavily for what could be years and years? It would have been easier, more natural, if she had known Catherine Cranshaw for all her life, as she had Cicely's great grandmother. If she married Abbot, Catherine would become family – when, not if, she reminded herself.

Melody's thoughts then wandered to how that would be, to live with Abbot and share everything with him. She was well educated in the ways of married couples; wooden dwellings with multiple generations inside hold few secrets. The sound of the motorcar as Roman drove out of the yard brought her out of her daydream. She had been relieved that he had not begged her to change her mind, or become angry that she had refused such a benevolent proposition.

Rolling onto her side, Melody began to pick at a stalk of straw that had worked its way through the blankets that covered the bales. If she had been married in Emmett there would have been a group of women to stitch her linen and help with her bridal frock. They would have prepared food and brought out the elderberry wine to bless the celebration. Cicely and her sisters would have helped Melody gather flowers to decorate the cabin or caravan that would be her new home.

But she was not in Emmett. A tear trickled down her nose and she angrily wiped it away with her sleeve. No good would come of wishing for what she could not have, she told herself.

Abbot returned to the farmhouse early that afternoon. He was soaked to the skin, as were all the men in the fields. It was part of running a farm that he would not miss at all if he managed to secure the legal secretary position. As his boots were caked in mud, he entered the farmhouse through the kitchen door and immediately turned into the washroom. Cook was taking her afternoon nap in her room, Agnes had her afternoon off, and the house was quiet and still. Abbot removed his boots and coat, dried his hair and face roughly with a hand towel that had been left over the back of a chair, then padded through the house and up to his bedroom leaving damp footprints behind him.

Cook's snores welcomed him as he reached the landing. Abbot wanted a bath; Cook would just have to put up with being woken by the groaning pipes if she had not put her earplugs in, he decided. He undressed and wrapped himself in his dressing gown. In the bathroom he let the hot tap run until it went cold again. There would be time for the water to heat up again before Cook needed any. He swirled some cold water into the tub, then dared to get in and risk a scalding. As he sunk into the water, he closed his eyes. It was almost as if he were in his own home at times like these. No one else to bother him; he could come and go as he pleased without needing to explain or excuse.

The hot water made his skin prickle as it turned red. A thought occurred to him that perhaps he had been hasty in asking Melody to marry him. Perhaps he should have struck out by himself and established himself in his occupation before asking her to join him. He could have lived the life of a bachelor, sampled a few of the pleasures that single men had at their fingertips. He smiled to himself; four months in France had opened his eyes to such pleasures. He did not think he would be missing out on anything now by taking a wife.

But would it be Melody? Would she choose him, or would she decide that Roman could offer her more. He certainly could, Abbot conceded. If that were her choice, he would put on a brave face and wish them well, no matter how shattered his dreams would be. Abbot sat up and splashed water onto his face; the thought of losing Melody to his brother was not one he wanted to dwell on.

What was she doing at that moment, he wondered as he began to wash off the day's grime. What was she thinking? He could never tell, even when he was with her and they were deep in conversation. She would say very little, allowing him to ramble on, his thoughts tumbling from his lips. Then she would comment, just a few words, but with such rapier-like precision it could take his breath away and turn him towards a new direction of thought he would never have considered without her.

He would do things properly, he told himself as he stood up and reached for a towel. He must see the vicar of Saint Michael's and have his best suit laundered. He stopped, one foot on the floor and the other still in the water: Melody would need a gown, and flowers, and they should have a party to celebrate, but where, and whom should they invite? Weddings were so much more than saying a few words at the altar he realised.

Having stayed after lunch to read to Catherine Cranshaw, Melody did not return to the farmhouse until her usual supper time. The rain was still falling and the evening light was fading fast under the weight of the clouds. Though the farmhouse had been connected to the electricity grid for some years, the servants' quarters were still often lit only by oil lamps. Melody took her seat at the servants' dining table after calling through to Cook that she had arrived.

Soon after Melody had sat down, Agnes bustled in carrying two plates of shepherd's pie with pale, boiled cabbage.

"Mister Roman's not back yet and Mister Abbot said he would see to the Missus, so I can eat this at a reasonable time for once!" Agnes put the plates down and poured herself some water. "I have some news for you," she said, looking at her plate and starting to blush.

Melody said nothing, but looked intently across the table, waiting for the revelation.

"Johnnie's had a raise! Only two shillings a week, but it will make all the difference. He told me last night; got down on one knee all proper and asked me to marry him. I said, 'Johnnie, but where shall we live?' and he said, 'Never you mind, but let's take a walk'. So walk we did, round the back of Jessop's, you know that track that goes along the edge of the stream and comes out at Fletcher's Cross?"

Melody nodded, her mouth full of cabbage.

"Just before you get to the dairy, there's a row of three cottages. Tiny they are, and the thatch is green and needs redoing but that's not important now. They're owned by the dairyman,

Ted Fellway. Johnnie's boss has been on good terms with Ted, and when he heard Johnnie was thinking of striking out somewhere else so as we could be married, he asked Ted if Johnnie and me could have one of the cottages. And Ted said yes as soon as one was empty!"

Agnes' smile was as broad as the Cheshire Cat's. In truth, she was doing her best to convince herself that the cottage was a splendid opportunity despite the sorry state of its roof and the large puddle that formed at the back door every time it rained. She had mentioned both things to Johnnie, as gently as she could. He had explained that he would dig out a proper drain and patch up the inside of the roof until something more permanent could be arranged, but didn't she think it would make a grand little home for the two of them? Agnes couldn't help but agree.

"I thought I heard the church bell tolling the other day," Melody said, blowing on her food to cool it.

"Yes, old mister Camus. He'd lived there for years. Used to work in the dairy on the cheeses. Still, he's got no relations that we know of, so we can have his furniture if we want it. That will save us a bob or two as well." She tucked into her own dinner with a spoon.

"When will you be married?"

"Soon as. We're to see the vicar this weekend. In a month I should think. It will be a pity to be after Michaelmas, but we have to wait three weeks as it is."

"And you'll keep working here?"

"Oh yes, at least until the kiddies come. The misters won't manage the missus by themselves; they'll need me to keep seeing to her for a while yet."

Melody swallowed her food slowly as the implications of Agnes' plans meshed with the future Abbot had painted for her.

The rain had temporarily stopped when Melody left by the kitchen door to return to the stable loft. An army of snails covered the path around the side of the house and try and she might to avoid them all, some fell under her boots with a sad, small, crunch. She had listened to Agnes' chatter about the cottage and the wedding plans for well over an hour longer than she usually would have. It had taken Cook's gruff comment about some people having all the time in the world to rouse Agnes back to her duties.

Abbot had been surprised at his mother's increased appetite. They had sat next to each other at the dining table, and frequently he had spooned more vegetables and meat onto her plate to prevent her from clumsily helping herself and spilling everything onto the tablecloth. As he ate his meal, Abbot talked of his plans. That evening, instead of no response at all from his mother, once or twice he found her looking at him as he spoke with what he was sure was comprehension of the topic. She still did not speak, nod or even smile at him, but she was looking at him and watching his mouth move. That was more attention than Catherine had shown her son in several years and he was thankful for it.

It did, however, cause him to wonder if her current state of needing infant-like care would always remain, or if she truly would return to her old self again if encouraged to mix with more people. Her old self; Abbot remembered Catherine as she had been, attentively reading the brothers stories or playing tennis on the lawn. Those days would never return but if his mother could make more of an effort to look after her own basic needs, perhaps around-the-clock care would not be required for her.

Abbot had been thinking through the expenses of taking on the cottage, and a wife as well as his mother living with them. Her small income would help but would not cover a full-time nurse. It had occurred to him while out in the fields that morning that he might be making a large assumption that Melody would simply take over where Agnes had been so efficient with his mother in recent years. Melody had spoken fondly of the elderly people of Emmett, but he realised now that fondness was not the same as having to care for them day after day, and perhaps during the night also.

The alternative was to leave Catherine at the farmhouse with Roman. Abbot knew she would come to no harm there, but would she prosper in the same way he hoped she would in the village? It seemed to him unlikely. As he wiped his mother's chin with a napkin to mop up some gravy, he could not imagine Roman doing the same for her. Roman would expect Agnes to look after Catherine.

After settling Catherine in the drawing room, Abbot took his cigarettes to the front door to smoke. He had always preferred not to smoke in front of his parents, and as Agnes had lit the fire in the drawing room, he wanted to feel the cooler night air on his face for a few moments. He also wondered if Melody was in the stable. He would be able to see her lantern light through the small window if she were there. Abbot chuckled as he opened the front door; where else would she be? He took a cigarette from the packet and looked up at the loft window. There was no light inside.

He was about to strike a match when he heard her footsteps on the path. Smiling he lit his cigarette and drew the smoke deeply in, flicking the match out onto the wet cobbles. Melody saw it fall to the ground and sizzle as the flame was extinguished. Her stomach gave an involuntary skip.

"You are out late tonight." Abbot leaned on the door frame.

"Agnes had a lot to say." *And has given me much to think about,* Melody thought to herself. She changed her usual route across the yard and stopped just beyond the porch. Close enough to see Abbot clearly, but out of arm's reach.

Abbot wanted to know if Melody had reached a decision, yet he did not want to pressure her into saying so if she was not ready to. Still, the question of his mother hung heavy on his shoulders.

"I have been thinking..."

"I may have been too presumptuous..."

They both spoke at once, then stopped. Abbot drew again on his cigarette then said, "After you."

Where others may have insisted it was quite all right, and that of course he should go first, Melody simply started again.

"I have been thinking about everything you've told me. About the house in Robey and your job, if you secure it, and your mother and marriage and all of it."

Abbot felt an icicle of fear in his chest. Had she chosen Roman? Was she about to let him down gently?

"Go on."

"Agnes is getting married but she needs to keep her job, and if your mother lives with us then Agnes won't be needed here and then she won't be able to afford to make the cottage nice for when the babies start coming, and ..."

"Wait a minute!" Abbot held up his hand to stop her. He pushed himself off the door frame and stepped forwards. "Are you saying you won't marry me because Agnes would lose her job, or are you saying you will marry me but we need to keep Agnes in employment?"

Melody was silent for a moment. The sound of a motorcar came through the night from the lane, the glow of the headlights showing hazily above the hedgerows. Abbot did not want this crucial conversation to be interrupted by the arrival of his brother.

Pulling the front door closed, he dropped his cigarette onto the cobbles and blew out the last of the smoke. "Shall we go to the stable? It's starting to rain again."

Melody allowed herself to be shepherded across the yard. She also did not want to be the cause of another confrontation between the brothers. Abbot allowed Melody to climb the ladder to the loft, then followed. Melody then lit her small storm lamp, turning the wick down low before replacing the glass cover and setting it on the stool she used as a table. The smell of paraffin briefly filled the air and one of the horses snorted its displeasure from the stalls. They listened to the car engine approaching, Melody sitting on her bed and Abbot standing at the top of the ladder. The motorcar drew into the yard. Its door opened and closed. Footsteps across the cobbles, then quiet again.

Abbot was reminded for a moment of a French farmhouse from his past, of a young woman of Melody's age who had stood defiantly and silently as he had pushed back some sacking used as curtains. Their eyes had met in the semi darkness. She had not looked at him with fear as so many of the women had; she had held her head up and stood her ground. Abbot had called over his shoulder that the store room was empty, and let the sacking fall back over the doorway. He had not remembered the woman again until that moment, seeing Melody's face set with resolution, watching him.

"May I sit?" Abbot's throat was dry after the cigarette. He would have liked a whisky but did not want to return to the house.

Melody shuffled along her bed to make room.

"Cecily would say I was being forward." There was no invitation in Melody's voice, only a shade of sadness.

"If you'd rather we go back outside, we can, though I can hear the rain."

"No, we're all right here."

"Very well. Let's see if we can work through any concerns you have over Agnes. You say she is to be married?"

"Johnnie had a raise in his wages and the butcher put in a word for them so they can take one of the dairy cottages."

"I see. Well, that wouldn't necessarily mean she would have to leave here, she's not a school teacher..."

"No, and she doesn't want to."

"But leaving you and I aside for a moment, if Mother were to leave the farm, are you concerned that my brother would have no need of Agnes?"

"It'd be only him in such a big house. He could do for himself with Cook making his meals."

Abbot gave a small smile. "I can't see Roman sweeping the floors or wrestling with the mangle, can you?"

"Why not? Granfer swept the cabin and kept it clean, we both did."

"We are not woodlanders, Melody. Though I see nothing wrong in it, I simply don't think it would occur to Roman until he was knee-deep in dust or found he had no clean shirts left. No, I think Agnes' position here is secure for as long as she wants it, though of course she will want to sleep in her own bed once she and Johnnie have their own home."

His words lingered between them. He wanted to take her hand and tell her that whatever she wanted from him, he would do his utmost to make it happen. He dared not. It was like herding the sheep, he realised; one wrong step, one unexpected movement and they would scatter in all directions.

Melody twisted a straw stalk between her fingers. They were forever working their way through the sheet and blanket she slept on. In the cabin her bed had been a wooden box with a leaf mattress topped with a feather and wool mattress to lay on. The leaves had to be replaced every year; it was one of the Emmett children's favourite occupations where they would pile up dry leaves and bracken to be used and hope no other children would run past and take a jump into another family's pile. It would be happening now, Melody realised, and the rain would not be welcome.

"Melody?"

She had not heard him.

"I was away..."

"I know," he said gently, "I can tell by your face when you are thinking of ... the past. I asked you, is there anything else you feel prevents us from marrying?"

"Who owns the land beyond the cottage?"

It was not what Abbot was expecting. "Do you mean between the village and the Derring road?"

"The hill at the back with the stand of Ash trees."

"I would have to enquire to be sure, but I think it would be either the Pursey farm or common land. Why?"

"I should like to walk there sometimes. Roman might not want me to walk in your woodland, and if he sells to the Commission then they might put up fences to keep people out. I need the trees." The last sentence, she almost whispered.

Abbot now took her hand in his. It was not smooth like Isobel's or her friends' with their creams and lotions. Melody's hands were always criss-crossed with scratches and stained from whatever plant or tree she had been working with. Her nails were bitten short; the quicks covering any sign of pale half-moons.

"I will find out who owns those trees. I know you have reservations. It is only natural to be nervous, but I believe we could have a wonderful future together, Melody. Will you say yes?"

Meeting the Neighbours

The Cranshaws were finishing breakfast when Agnes brought the first post into the dining room. Roman flicked through his envelopes and selected one from the Forestry Commission. Abbot watched his brother's face break into a rare smile as he read the typed words on cream notepaper.

"Good news, brother?"

"Indeed. We have reached an agreement. The Commission will take on the woodland south of Purchase Field, leaving us with the small parcel of trees by Ribble Top. Better access for them to the Derring road."

"Congratulations. Ahh…"

"Something of importance for you too?"

"The solicitors in Derring … they are pleased to offer me the position of legal secretary while I continue my training. That's a relief! Everything is falling into place, Mother." He looked at Catherine who was munching on her third slice of buttered toast. She looked at him but said nothing. The very act of acknowledging his voice was enough to bring an even bigger smile to Abbot's face.

"Everything?" Roman had assumed that Melody would agree to marry Abbot in time as she had turned down his offer, yet the finality of hearing it was not something he welcomed.

"Yes! Melody has agreed to be my wife. There is so much to prepare, so many arrangements to make, and with this..." he waved the solicitor's letter about "...I shall have much less time to accomplish it all in. Do you plan to use the motorcar today?"

"No, though you should check the oil before you go very far in it. I think we may have a leak somewhere. I was going to take a better look this afternoon, but it should be safe enough to drive."

"Excellent, I have several people to see now that things are properly in motion."

After Abbot had left the stable loft the previous evening, Melody had remained sitting on her bed for some time. She had half expected him to possess her once she had agreed to marry him; she had mentally prepared herself for it. Yet he had simply kissed her hand, which he had been holding for some minutes, then wished her a good night and had left. Melody felt as though a weight had been lifted from her, but at the same time, an emptiness still remained. A wedding should be a joyous time; she had only Agnes to share it with and Agnes was already full of her own plans and preparations.

Slowly Melody stood and undressed. She turned out the lamp and went to bed for what she realised would now be only a limited number of nights. She would have a real bed again. She would have her own kitchen. Her own chairs and table. It would not be in a cabin or a caravan, but the cottage need not be cluttered and stifling as she had felt houses to be. Melody went to sleep thinking of the things she would make from wood for her new home. She slept well that night.

Agnes' reaction when Melody told her the news the next day was less enthusiastic than Melody had hoped.

"When is the wedding going to happen?" Agnes was folding wet sheets so they would fit through the mangle and Melody had offered to help.

"Abbot says as soon as he can arrange it all. He will take the cottage from the first of October, and he starts at the solicitors' office on Monday."

"So it might not be for a while then, if he's busy with his new position," Agnes brightened at the prospect of a delay.

"I don't know. He said we have to see the vicar together."

"Oh yes," now Agnes assumed the authority of one who had been through the experience, "yes, Johnnie and me went Wednesday evening to see him. He'll give you a good talking to, to make sure you believe all the right things. Then he'll ask you about the choir and bell ringers and give you the date. Don't you have weddings in church in Emmett?"

"Not always. Some people do, but I've never been to one."

Agnes raised an eyebrow; perhaps Cook was right, the wood-landers were strange. "What happens then, if two people want to get married or whatever you call it?"

"The elders and the families have to agree, then they help build a cabin or get a caravan and help with the things to go in it. When it's ready the two families eat together and then the man and woman just go to their new home." It didn't feel to Melody that there was anything wrong with that arrangement, but she could see Agnes did not approve.

"It wouldn't feel right to me, not to have God's blessing. Johnnie hasn't had so much as a kiss off me yet, and he won't until that ring is on my finger."

Melody couldn't help blushing. She had never thought of kisses as being promiscuous, but Agnes' words made her realise the gulf between their experiences. Luckily the laundry room was hot and steamy and both girls were already red-faced.

"What are you going to wear?" Agnes held the first sheet up to the mangle rollers and waited for Melody to begin turning the handle.

"Abbot said he would take me to Derring for a new outfit. He said he can get a new shirt for himself when he has his lunchtime."

"There's a dressmaker on Clement Road in Derring, she is very reasonable and would make you a frock."

"Is that where you will have yours made up?"

"Oh no, I have been saving up, I have a fitting next Wednesday in Derring with missus McKinley."

If Agnes had expected surprise or even jealousy from Melody, she hid it well. Mrs McKinley was a well-known dressmaker who had run the sewing room for a design house in Bristol for many years. She also happened to be a contributor to the girl's training school where Agnes had been placed. Melody had never heard of Mrs McKinley.

Agnes changed the subject. "Will you come down to the dance tomorrow?"

Melody looked blankly at Agnes.

"The dance in Robey church hall. For Michaelmas. It's the end of the celebrations this week. Missus Pennard won three shillings at the whist drive on Tuesday night. Wait, let me fold this one again, it's slipped. It's the Women's Institute harvest lunch today, Missus Pennard is taking her pea and marrow soup."

"Michaelmas sounds like our Candlemas week."

"We don't have the travelling folk come for Michaelmas. The vicar wouldn't allow it."

"The showmen will be beyond Audling at this time of year. There's a big horse fair, Granfer went one year with some of the other men." A sudden wave of grief welled up in Melody's chest and caught her by surprise. She could not stop the tears and fumbled in her apron pocket for a handkerchief.

Agnes lay the end of the wet sheet over the top of the mangle roller and reached out to Melody to give her a hug. Melody surrendered and sobbed for a few moments on Agnes' shoulder. Eventually she composed herself and they stepped back from each other so that Melody could wipe her face and blow her nose.

"It's not easy, having no family," Agnes observed quietly.

"Will you come?"

"To your wedding? To mister Abbot?"

"Yes, will you come?"

"I don't know ... I'm staff, I don't know that mister Abbot would want staff there..."

"I want you there Agnes, I don't have anyone else. Please?"

"Well, I should want you to come to my wedding too, although..." Agnes hesitated, unsure of how to explain that she had not anticipated having to invite one of her employers also. "Mister Abbot might not want to come."

"Oh, he would. We both will. But you and Johnnie will come to ours."

Agnes could not refuse Melody's big, pleading eyes. They continued with the laundry, chatting about Agnes' arrangements. Melody tried to absorb everything Agnes told her; she assumed Abbot would have similar ideas about how a wedding should be and she wanted to do what was expected of her. She realised that Abbot's happiness was becoming more important to her.

Meanwhile Agnes frequently had to curb her jealousy of Melody's good fortune. She did not want to be jealous; she genuinely liked Melody and had enjoyed having another woman closer to her own age around the farm. Yet she could not help feeling annoyed that while Melody would be living in a pretty house on the edge of Robey and would not have to continue her employment, Agnes would be living in a tiny cottage opposite a noisy, odorous dairy, and would have to walk to and from the farm every day rather than only on Wednesdays as she currently did.

When Melody offered to take the sheets out to the washing line, Agnes was grateful. Then, when alone in the laundry room, she emptied the large washtub and gave herself a talking to. She did not want to marry either of the Cranshaw brothers, and if she and Johnnie worked and saved hard, they would be able to move to a better home in time. She was lucky to be marrying anyone at all, she reminded herself, given her mother's situation and the outnumbering of women to men in her generation.

"A dance? Do you want to go?" Abbot had returned from his errands and Melody was wating for him on the bench outside the stable. The sky overhead was heavy with grey clouds but in the west a brighter pale strip separated if from the hills.

"Agnes said it would be good for me to meet some more of the villagers."

"Well, of course it would be, but do you want to?" Abbot was thinking of Melody's reaction to his friends some weeks before.

Although the villagers were far removed in class and habit from Isobel's set, he thought it might be a lot for Melody to take in all at once.

Melody had been giving the occasion much thought that afternoon. When she had gone in to read to Catherine Cranshaw, she had been surprised to see the woman with an open book in her lap. True, Catherine was still in her usual chair and gazing out at the garden, but it had been the first time Melody had seen her holding anything other than food or cutlery. Melody felt sure that very slowly, Catherine was returning from the dark place she had retreated to after David's death. If she could do that, Melody could leave her dark place behind also and make new friends in the village.

"I would like to."

"Then we shall go. But if you want to leave, just say the word. Even if we've only had one dance. These village affairs can be rather slow things. Now, I still have a few things to arrange tomorrow, but on Saturday, what say you that we go into Derring and look out a frock for you?"

"Agnes said there is a place that would make me something."

"That may be so, but there is an outfitters' on the high street who may have just the thing you could bring away on the day. I need some new shirts in any case, and we have an account there, so I think it's where we should begin."

Melody agreed without protest. Shopping for clothes was something she had only done on two or three occasions before and that had meant travelling on the barge down to Wynnham with Avens. She had never been in a motorcar and was a little nervous of it. Melody would have been more willing to walk down to the village and catch the bus to Derring, but Abbot intended to make full use of the car while he had the opportunity.

He would spend enough time on the buses when he began his job at the solicitor's office, he told her.

The opportunity for a short ride in the motorcar came the following evening as the rain once again poured down over Wynn Vale. Agnes had permission to take leave from her evening duties, and sat with Melody in the back seat of the vehicle as Abbot waited for one of the farm hands to crank the engine. They made their way along the lane, taking precisely six minutes to arrive outside the church hall where Johnnie was sheltering in the porch.

Once inside, Melody was acutely aware that her outfit was not in the fashionable style of the village women. She watched self-consciously as the couples circled the floor, but could not avoid joining the dance forever. Eventually Abbot coaxed her out into the throng, and led her gently around for several circuits as she tried to both avoid his feet but furtively glance around her at the same time. They stopped and clapped at the end of the song, and Melody asked for a drink as an excuse to leave the dancefloor for a while.

The evening was a pleasant one. Agnes introduced Melody to some more of the villagers, and once word got round that she and Abbot would be moving into the cottage at the end of the village, many more people came to make themselves known to the couple. Abbot was interested in the activities that his mother could take part in. The chairwoman of the Women's Institute insisted that Catherine Cranshaw would be welcome to their meetings even if she simply sat and said nothing.

The vicar made a short appearance at the dance, to announce the amount raised as contributions to the electricity installation at the church. He then swiftly retreated, not wanting his wife to drag him out onto the dance floor. At ten o'clock the last waltz was played, and the lights in the main room were turned on.

"Did you enjoy yourself?" Agnes asked Melody as they climbed back into the motor car.

"The people were kind. At least I will know some of them when we live here."

"I expect you'll have plenty of visitors," Agnes said with a knowing look. It would not take the village women long to find some reason or other to call at the cottage and see how Melody was getting along. There had been some whispered conversations that evening about people from Emmett and Melody's old-fashioned clothes.

The trip to Derring was almost too overwhelming for Melody. Where Wynnham was a small, quiet town where most people kept to themselves, Derring was ever striving to rival its bigger cousins Audling, and Prestport in the east of Wynn Vale for the variety of shops and entertainments it could offer. Abbot had kept the errands he had to run close to his chest on Friday, but insisted on driving to Derring so that they would be able to transport their purchases back with them and not arrange delivery.

The sun tried hard to give some warmth, and the trees had turned golden-orange almost overnight. The streets were dotted with puddles, causing many shoppers to skip and jump over them, occasionally bumping into each other with a good-natured apology. Melody noted how the people of Derring liked to laugh and shake hands when they met. She had imagined the town to be dark and dirty with industry from Abbot's descriptions, but found it light and bright with the last of the flower displays in the Municipal Gardens spelling out the King and Queen's names. The shop windows had colourful displays; Abbot chattered on to Melody endlessly about the things they would need for the cottage and pointed them out as they passed each new shop in the High Street.

They had lunch in a small café, at a table in the window. Melody peeked over the top of the lace half-curtains and could see the townspeople passing by. Abbot watched her watching them for a moment while they waited for their meal.

"What do you think of the place?" he asked.

"It's very bright. Everyone seems happy here."

"They work hard. Almost as if they want to prove they are as good as Audling."

"Why should they need to prove it?"

"I suppose a little pride. Being only a little smaller, I suppose they feel they should be treated with equal importance. You've never had brothers or sisters, so perhaps you're not familiar with how it can feel, to be overlooked because of your age or status."

Melody turned from the window to look at Abbot.

"I've learned a lot since I left Emmett. Some people worry more about what strangers think of them, than the people who care for them. Some people should talk more, and others should talk a lot less. And that I am happy on my own, but I don't always want to be."

"I want you to be happy with me, Melody. I shall try not to inhibit you, or expect you to do things you are not comfortable with. I know your ... freedom is important to you. I understand that more now than ever."

"People might talk about you, for marrying me."

"Let them. I can build my reputation as a lawyer here in Derring. The people of Robey know me, they know our family. I can't see that a little gossip would do any real harm."

The waitress brought their lunch and conversation turned to more practical wedding-related things. When they left the café, Abbot left Melody at a small women's outfitters where she was measured, appraised, and tried on a variety of dresses and separates. The assistant assembled two piles of clothes, the prices of one she made out a bill for when Abbot returned.

There still remained the question of where Catherine Cranshaw would live. Abbot had been correct in his assumption that even if their mother did live with him, Roman would require both Cook and Agnes to continue in their positions at the farm. Melody stayed in the stable loft, despite the night temperatures dipping lower with each passing week, but worked less on her baskets and wooden carvings. Instead, she spent more time with Catherine while trying to keep out of Roman's way. That was not difficult; Roman had taken to driving to Audling two or three times a week without giving any details of what he was doing there.

Cook had not commented on the news of the wedding. This, Agnes assured Melody, meant that Cook approved of the arrangement. Melody was less certain. She had already agreed with Abbot that after the ceremony in the church, their guests would reassemble at the village hall for some light refreshments. The vicar's wife had offered to provide the sandwiches and sausage rolls for a very reasonable fee. It occurred to Melody that Cook might be upset at this.

Leaving Catherine Cranshaw in the drawing room one afternoon, Melody went along to find Cook in the kitchen. Cook was peeling potatoes which would sit in water while she had her afternoon rest.

Before Melody could speak, Cook began, "You needn't think I'll be taking any instruction from you once you're Mrs Cranshaw, my girl." Cook continued to peel the potatoes, not taking her eyes from the paring knife.

"I shan't be living here when I'm married to Abbot."

"Just as well."

Melody swallowed. "Roman and Mrs Cranshaw will still need you. And Agnes. Will you come to the hall after the wedding?"

Cook stopped peeling and looked across the table at Melody. "For fish paste sandwiches and weak tea? If the Churchwomen's Guild teas are anything to go by, that's what Mrs Callow will serve up. And her so-called Victoria Sponge, well..." Cook sniffed and left the sentence hanging between them. Then she returned to the potatoes.

"Would you please make us a cake? Agnes says that wedding breakfasts should have an iced fruit cake, but I don't know that Mrs Callow would be able to make one for us."

"It would be over-cooked and dry with the fruit all on the bottom if she did! Iced, you say. Nothing fancy, not enough time to feed it well. But I suppose as I'll be making the Christmas cake on Friday, I could double the quantities without too much trouble. Mister Abbot always did like my fruit cakes."

"They are delicious. You are by far the best cook I have ever known."

Cook looked at Melody, searching for any trace of a smirk on her face but found none. Satisfied the compliment was well meant, she nodded in agreement. Melody had never known any other cooks employed as such. The woodlanders of Emmett were not known for their baking or confectionary; they ate simply and often kept a stew pot going for days by adding water and whatever could be caught or picked and brought back to the cabins. The closest most woodlanders came to making cakes were the small plain scones made with flour, a little fat, and fresh herbs that were cooked on flat tin trays and served with the stew.

"Bonfire night too. Not something you people mark, I imagine."

Melody risked sitting at the table. "They have a fire in Emmett Green, but we don't in the wood, no."

"You could make yourself useful and make some sticks for the toffee apples. We always send some down to the village for the kiddies on bonfire nights."

"I can do that. And then it will be Christmas. What do people do here then?"

"What do you mean, what do they do?"

"I've seen that Michaelmas is important to Robey. In Emmett, we don't mark Christmas unless we go to the farms where they do. Candlemas is when we celebrate getting through the winter, although it's not right at the end of winter."

"I seem to remember hearing you people work on farms around Wynn Vale in the summers. I expect they celebrate Christmas in much the same way that we do. Church in the morning, or at midnight if you're that devout, then a good lunch with presents afterwards and parlour games. A bit of a sing song in the evening or a recital. Of course it won't be the same with Mister Abbot living elsewhere."

ALL'S WELL THAT ENDS WELL

Saturday 5 November 1927 was a dark and blustery day. The parish councillors had met the day before and all agreed that if the pyramid of old wood on the patch of ground behind the dairy were to be lit, some kind of accelerant would be needed. It had been growing daily through October, the result of the yearly clear out of old and broken furniture by the villagers, and had been drenched almost daily by the heavens.

Abbot stood at the window of the kitchen in the cottage, a cup of coffee in one hand and a slice of bread and dripping in the other. He was gazing out on the sodden and stripped garden. In a few hours, Melody would be his wife. They would be sharing the cottage, and the following spring his mother would join them. It had been a difficult conversation with Roman, but Abbot felt that the outcome was the best for them all. It would give Melody time to make the cottage a comfortable home, he would have time to establish himself in his new position, and the better weather would encourage his mother to attend the various activities available in the village. Yes, all in all, it was the best decision for all of them.

Roman joined Abbot at the window, with his own cup of coffee.

"I should have driven down. I shall be soaked before I reach the farm."

"I'm glad you stayed here last night. I know I've been on my own here for a month now, but it was good to have some company. Thank you once again for all the to-ing and fro-ing you'll be doing today."

"Not at all. It would have been churlish of me to refuse. Run me through the itinerary again, just so I can be absolutely sure of where I need to be and when."

"I thought you could bring Mother and Cook down first, which will give Cook time to add her cake to the spread in the church hall, and for Mother to be got into the church. Mrs Callow will stay with Mother there while you go back up to fetch Agnes and Melody in time for the ceremony to begin at eleven."

"And you are confident that everyone else will have arrived by then?" Roman raised an eyebrow at the swaying bushes in the garden.

"James and Isobel are staying in Derring and will be driving over. And the others I imagine will be leaving shortly. I do hope Melody appreciates my endeavours."

Melody was brushing her hair in the bathroom of the farmhouse. She had reluctantly agreed to stay in Abbot's old room the night before, after Agnes explained it would be easier for her to get ready without then being wind-blown and soaked crossing the yard. Sleep had come in the early hours, and she yawned wide at her reflection.

Agnes herself was busy with Catherine Cranshaw, and Cook was making bread at the kitchen table. Melody began to braid her hair in the way Emmett brides-to-be traditionally wore. She had bought some lengths of ribbon in Derring and used them to weave through her braids and tie up the ends. Despite Agnes' encouragement, Melody had declined to have her hair cut into a more fashionable shorter style. On the dressing table, Avens' wooden hair comb with its amber stone lay waiting.

The outfit she had chosen was laid on the bed. White was a wholly unsuitable colour for women of the wood; only underclothes were made from white linen or cotton, but even these were generally dyed with plants so that any marks were less noticeable. Melody had, at the insistence of the outfitter's assistant, picked out a white cotton blouse with a rounded collar. She had spent some time embroidering leaves and flowers around the collar and cuffs to make it her own. This she would wear with a dark moss green woollen skirt, and a short dark green riding jacket that flared with a peplum at the back.

Instead of a veil, Melody had chosen a small green straw hat, in a style often called a 'Mary' as it was favoured by servants on their days off around Wynn Vale. Agnes had carefully stitched some paper flowers around the brim, while tutting every now and then at its inappropriateness as bridal attire. The rest of Melody's possessions had been packed into her kit bag and now stood in the corner of the back bedroom at the cottage, along with a half-finished basket and a bundle of soaked willow whips.

Cook's cake was safely enclosed in a large, upturned tin. Though she had grumbled at the extra baking and icing required of her, she was proud of how it now looked. The Christmas cake remained uniced, in a separate tin, to be fed each week with a large spoonful of brandy. Cook sat in the front seat of the motor car with the cake tin clasped on her lap, as Roman shepherded his mother into the rear seat.

Catherine Cranshaw had eaten a hearty breakfast, and allowed Agnes to dress her with little fuss. Agnes had picked out a plain winter frock with woollen stockings and a thick winter coat with a russet fur collar. Once dressed, Catherine was led back downstairs in her coat, to wait for Roman to arrive. Agnes had left Catherine in the drawing room for only a few moments, when she discovered the older woman in the hallway, attempting to open the front door. It was clear that Catherine understood the significance of the coat, and it took Agnes much persuasion to get her to return to the drawing room to wait. On her way back upstairs, Agnes pushed the top bolt across on the front door, just in case.

The village turned out to witness the ceremony dressed in their almost finest clothes. The Cranshaws were almost one of their own; Melody was an exotic novelty who, despite making a good impression at the Michaelmas dance, was certainly not one of their own. The whole arrangement of players had caused much interest. Mrs Callow had innocently mentioned at a coffee morning that Roman would not be Abbot's best man, and then to cover her indiscretion, had felt it necessary to explain to those gathered that Abbot's friend James would be the best man and Roman would actually be giving Melody away. The raised eyebrows around the group would have dislodged hats had the women been wearing any.

For the Cranshaws it had made sense. Melody had no older male relative. Roman had realised the need for such a role before Abbot, and had suggested he take that place. As Roman pulled the motor car to the side of the lane in front of St Michael's church, he glanced at Melody who sat up straight in the passenger seat.

"Are you ready?"

"I am." Melody turned her head slowly towards Roman.

Had Agnes not been at that point waiting outside of the motor car, holding the small posy of Honesty seed pods, Teasles and brown beech leaves that Melody had assembled, this story could have had a very different ending. Roman Cranshaw could have restarted the engine. Melody could have remained in the passenger seat. The pair could have returned to the farmhouse and ridden out the storm of hostility which would certainly have blown up around them for such scandalous disregard for family loyalty.

Agnes tapped on the passenger door window impatiently.

"It's starting to rain again. We should hurry and get you inside!"

In their rush to enter the church, Melody did not see the large wagon with the two grey Percheron horses tethered a little way along the lane. It was only as she took Roman's arm and began her slow walk up the aisle that she recognised Cecily and some other Emmett woodlanders in the congregation at the rear of the church. Melody's smile was as wide as the river Wynn as she reached Abbot's side in front of the Reverend Callow.

"Did you see your friends?" Abbot whispered, knowing that she must have done.

"How did they know to come?"

The vicar cleared his throat.

"I'll explain later."

"How you all find your way through the woods is still a mystery to me!" Abbot laughed as someone passed him another brown bottle of beer.

"You should have seen him, Mel! Wandering around making such a noise. We watched him for a good while before Ambrose stepped out onto the path in front of him and asked him what he was doing there." Cecily sat across the small table from Melody and Abbot, with her brother who had driven the cart down that morning.

"It's a good thing he did. I might still be wandering there lost now!"

"No, you were getting close to the river. We'd have not let you fall in." Ambrose picked up one of the sandwich triangles from the laden plate in front of him and pushed the whole thing into his mouth. Cecily scowled and elbowed him in the ribs, causing Ambrose to stop mid-chew and consider his social *faux pas*.

Melody chuckled. She felt so much more relaxed now that the ceremony was over and she was among her own people again. She could ignore the glances and longer stares of the villagers, safe in the knowledge that she was now Mrs Cranshaw of Wynnlowe Cottage, Robey. That Cecily and the others had travelled to be with her on her wedding day meant so much more than she could put into words. She knew she would still be unlikely to return to Emmett, the elders would not want her to revisit the shame of being turned out on the community, but she had not been completely disowned by her people. That Cecily had also brought Avens' kitchenware had caused Melody more tears, but this time joyous ones.

Cecily looked bright-eyed and rosy-cheeked in her best dress of dark brown, and had confided in Melody as soon as they had a few moments alone that she thought she was expecting a baby. She would have her own cabin the following spring with Tam Oakley in his family's clearing. Tam worked at the paper mill; Cecily felt they might not stay long in the wood if Tam could make up to foreman with the extra shillings that would bring.

"He wants to move out to Wynnlea. Got his eye on a cottage, he says."

"You'll leave the wood."

"We all will in time. Wynnlea has a nice little school, and to have a bath and a proper toilet will be worth moving away for."

Melody realised how much she had grown to enjoy indoor plumbing since leaving Emmett. It was the people she missed, not the deprivations of the cabins and caravans.

The wedding reception lasted for most of the afternoon. There was dancing, and speeches, as tradition dictated. Abbot thanked everyone at least three times, and made a point of mentioning Cook's baking efforts. Johnnie joined the party just after two, as the butcher had opened as usual that morning. He and Abbot talked of what would be needed to do up the dairy cottage, and Abbot offered to help on any weekend if he could. Johnnie was a little in awe of the Cranshaws and beamed with pride as he told Agnes later of his new friendship.

Having fulfilled his duties as best man, James stayed with his sister on the edge of the celebrations. Roman joined them for a while, giving Isobel a chance to invite him to stay with them in the new year. There was a twinkle in her eye that Roman did not ignore.

Catherine Cranshaw had not smiled as much in a very long while. She still did not speak, but she ate some of the food placed before her and watched the villagers swirling around as the dancing began and even clapped her hands gently in time with the music. Agnes sat with her in a corner for a while, then gave up her seat to Cook who brought two of her village friends with their cups of tea. They chattered away as if Catherine were not there, but she did not seem to mind. She was breathing in the abundance of energy and enjoyment in the church hall as if it were some medicated vapour.

When Roman decided he had socialised enough, he went to say goodbye to Abbot and Melody and collect Cook and his mother for the journey back to the farm. They all made their way to the little porch outside the church hall, then Abbot cranked the motor car's engine while Roman sat in the driver's seat.

"You make sure you collect my tin at the end of all this. I shall be wanting it back, and not see it in the next jumble sale." Cook buttoned her coat and prepared to launch herself down the path to the waiting car.

"I will. Thank you for coming." Melody turned to Catherine and took her porcelain-like hand. "And thank you too. We shall see you again very soon."

Abbot and Cook crossed on the path as he trotted back to see his mother down to the car.

"Happy." Catherine whispered, gripping Melody's hand as tightly as she could for a moment.

Abbot looked at Melody in surprise. Melody smiled, patted the woman's hand and gently encouraged her to go with Abbot. She waited in the porch for him to return once more.

"She spoke! It's been years since I heard Mother say anything at all. How did you manage that?"

"She's been getting better slowly all year."

"You have some magical touch, Melody." Abbot took her in his arms. "I believe every day will be the best day of my life from now on, with you."

Those who were closest to the door broke out into applause as the couple kissed. Three cheers were raised, then Abbot led Melody back into the hall for one final dance.

The end.

If you have enjoyed this tale, please do leave a rating or review on Amazon or Goodreads – and tell your friends!
Thank you.